THE

CRYING

SEA

To my friends at the
Qawra Palace Hotel
Teddy Cummins

This is a superb read and a story that will remain with you forever. Paddy Cummins captures so many moods in his telling of this tragedy, you feel you are there with the central characters. And because it's relating to a true story, it's even more poignant. You'll find it difficult not to cry at certain parts.

It's true that at times, the sea shows no mercy; the tension is built up so well here that you won't know until the time is right whether or not the sea needs more souls. This is a book and a story, which will travel and will be read and told when we are all long gone.

Damien Tiernan.

Author of "Souls Of The Sea"

Inspired by a true sea disaster…
A harrowing story of intense
human drama.

THE
CRYING
SEA

Paddy Cummins

BRIDGE
Publishing

ISBN 0–9538419-4-4

Printed in Ireland by :   Emco Printers,
                           New Ross,
                           Co. Wexford.

Cover photo: Beatriz Guerrero Gonzalez-Valerio.

BRIDGE PUBLISHING
Campile Co. Wexford. Ireland.
www.bridgepublishing.net

Dedicated to the people of Malta for their kindness and hospitality and for treating me as one of their own.

"I do not know what I should choose. I am caught in this dilemma: I want to be gone and be with Christ, which would be much the better, but for me to stay alive in this body is a more urgent need for your sake"

(Philippians I: 20 – 24.27)

The Crying Sea

Prologue

The little harbour, Blugarr Bay, is all eyes and ears as the elegant 'St Agatha' sails smoothly in to her berth. Her streamlined curves in rich cream and blue, her silky purring engine and her graceful presence says this is a serious boat, and the close-knit fishing folk are pleased for Paul Gauci and his family. There is no fanfare - Paul wouldn't approve – but in his heart a spark of hope glimmers; he feels a warm glow of gratitude to God for making this day possible.

The crossing from Sicily in his new trawler, with his retired father proudly sharing the helm, is the fulfilment of his dream. The blue water that surrounds Malta yields a rich harvest for those that can reap it. His father, grandfather and great-grandfather toiled and lived, but though excellent fishermen, were denied access to the real gold, for want of the means to reach it.

For Paul, a fit, ambitious thirty-five-year-old, slaving with inadequate equipment is not an option for the future. His wife and two young sons deserve the best he can give them. Perhaps the boys, like their father, will want no other life but the sea. He has thought long and hard about that. Sure…fine. But when they are ready, they must be given a future. Today the seed is being planted. With faith and confidence he can see it grow and flourish in the years ahead.

The colourful little luzzu, 'Santa Marie', having faithfully provided for the family since before he was born, will now be retired and have a well-deserved rest. Perhaps his father will use her occasionally for a bit of fun; it would be good for both of them.

As Paul steps ashore, he is surprised, but happy to see a little welcome party on the pier. Gabriella, glowing with pride and exuberance, rushes forward to give her husband a big kiss, Leo and Dom can't wait to hug their father.

Paul's younger brother, Jason, and his cousin Angelo, both fishermen who already share a similar trawler, joyously shake his hand before jumping aboard for a tour of inspection.

*

Back home, it's time for a little celebration. Drinks are on the house. Brandy for Grandpa, beer for Paul, Jason and Angelo, wine for Mummy; coke for Leo and Dom.

The conversation is ranging far and wide over the blue Mediterranean, from lucrative swordfishing grounds to lines of lampuki floats and tuna beds. The challenges and opportunities of Paul's new horizon are discussed and measured. Jason and Angelo present a rosy progress report on their success since acquiring *their* new boat, 'The Blue Horizon'. Grandpa, a lean, hardy sixty-seven-year-old, is delighted for Paul and his family. But he would love to be young again to harvest the rich waters that 'St Agatha' will make accessible. Gabriella prays that the large loan acquired to purchase the boat won't be a millstone around their necks.

"Please God it won't," prays Grandpa, "the fish are there, the market is good, and now you have the equipment to catch them."

Dom is tired. It's been a long day. He is only six. Before he goes to bed he has an important question for Dad.

"Dad, when you go to fish all these faraway places, will you be away then for a very long time?"

Paul feels a little sting in his heart but tries to conceal it.

"Ah, maybe a little longer, but you'll have Mummy to look after you. 'St. Agatha' has phones too, and sure we can have lots of talk when I'm away."

Dom is not entirely happy. Dad at home is better than Dad on the phone.

"I don't mind, Dad, if you're away for a long time, 'cause I'll be with you," Leo enthuses. Small for his age, active and intelligent, he is shaping to be like his father, strong and stocky. After months of bargaining, he has secured a promise from his mother that after his 'Confirmation' he can go fishing with Dad, but only during the school holidays.

"Now Leo," warns his mother, "you are only eleven. You can only go the odd time, your books come first."

"Ah Mummy, you know I want to be a good fisherman when I grow up and I have to learn."

He turns his pleading eyes towards his Dad. Paul understands. He well remembers his own boyhood days. His fascination with the sea and fishing was all-embracing. Leo is filled with the same burning ambition.

"Yes, Leo, you can come, but not every trip is suitable for a young boy. It's tough out there; sometimes only men are able for it."

"Now," said Mummy, "like a good boy, go to bed with Dom; he is very sleepy."

Reluctantly, with matters not entirely clarified, he says goodnight and both boys climb the stairs.

*

Overlooking the picturesque little harbour of Blugarr is the ornate red-domed parish church. It is dedicated to Our Lady,

Mother of Sorrows, Today it is festooned, colourful, full of joy and celebration. Confirmation Day is always a special occasion, a day of rest for the fishing boats and joyous festivities for the community.

Among the class of forty-five little 'Cadets', resplendent and ready to become 'Soldiers' in the 'Army of Christ' is Leo. He has been looking forward to this day for years. He sees it as a kind of graduation, a slipway from the shore of boring catechism, to the sea of fun and adventure with his dad on the new fishing boat.

For Paul and Gabriella, the torch of pride and happiness is burning brightly in their hearts. It's a beautiful day, a special family occasion to savour and cherish.

Dom is happy too, thinking of his own big day in a few years time, when *he* will be star of the show. Grandpa, uncles, aunts and cousins are all here to celebrate Leo's big day and digital cameras are set and ready to record every twist and turn.

It takes the bishop two hours to complete the ceremony, congratulate the children, parents and teachers and now he is chatting to the new 'Soldiers' while the group photograph is being organised.

"This is Leo" says Father Borg, introducing him to the bishop.

"Well done, Leo! You look splendid in your beautiful new suit. And what would *you* like to be when you grow up?"

"A fisherman, my lord."

"A fisherman!! Great! Just like the Apostles, Peter and Andrew."

The parish priest interjected. "Leo will be the fourth generation of his family to follow a career in fishing."

"Well Leo," said the bishop, "I wish you all God's blessings, and you will have new strength after to-day."

God's 'new army' line up for a picture with the bishop, priest and teachers, then for the treasured little family group photos.

Leo says he would like a special photo of Grandpa and himself. They pose, and their smiling eyes testify to a special mutual love and happiness.

The restaurants along the promenade are all buzzing with extra business. The 'Harbour View' is ready to welcome Leo's party for the celebration meal. They will relax, enjoy and savour the occasion. Later the extended family will disperse, while Paul, Gabriella, Dom and Grandpa will accompany Leo to the special treat he is really looking forward to: visiting the gigantic Marine Park in Sliema. The boys are good swimmers and can't wait to enjoy Malta's 'Disney' on water. It's Grandpa's gift to his favourite grandson on his special day. Leo is thrilled.

*

"How about a little celebration drink, Gabriella?"

"Why not, Paul. This is great, I can't believe it."

"Thank God, I hope it continues."

Paul rises from the table, now covered with invoices, statements, and a few substantial 'Fish Company' cheques.

They are reviewing the first three months of 'St Agatha' in their quiet kitchen. Grandpa has taken the boys to the pool.

He opens a bottle of red wine for his wife, uncaps a long cold beer for himself. They pour, kiss and touch glasses. Gabriella displays that impish smile.

"To 'St Agatha'" Paul toasts.

"To *Paul,* 'St. Agatha' and her crew," replies Gabriella.

"To the most clever and attractive woman in the world." Paul raises his glass again.

They lock eyes, smile and drink.

"You are really happy with the trawler, Paul?"

"Sure. It's a new life."

"And the crew?"

"Great. Mario is a brilliant fisherman, and a real warm, generous fellow too."

"Pity he never found a nice partner; he is such a good lad."

"Ah he might yet. He's only thirty."

"Perhaps he has no interest in women."

"Right now Mario has two priorities in his life: looking after his poor ailing mother and fishing. I can see him eventually having his own trawler. Caring for his mother is a big burden for him at present."

"How is young Ali coming along? Still getting sea sick?"

"He's amazing, never sick now and a great worker. For a teenager, a Somalia refugee and been through so much, he's great, always smiling and happy. I'm delighted with him."

"Brilliant, and a real handsome young fellow too."

"I think we'll have another look at the 'Master Plan'," suggests Paul.

"Okay. But it's working so well, it hardly needs changing."

They open the file.

Before taking the giant leap of acquiring the 'St Agatha' they had their plans well thought out. The bank, agreeing with the projections, was happy to come on board. Now it's delivery time and judging by the first three months; it's looking great. With average luck and fish prices holding up, they should easily reach and perhaps even exceed their targets. There's just one more week left to hunt the big swordfish and then it's time to harvest the juicy little lampuki. This should provide excitement and funding to Christmas and allow a leisurely stroll through the dodgy winter weather. The hot sun of April, May and June brings up the majestic tuna. Paul will be out there, ready to welcome them aboard the St 'Agathy'.

For the rest of summer they will be returning west to renew

acquaintance with their old combatant: the intrepid swordfish. A year ahead full of promise and opportunity, a whole new exciting challenge.

The boys and their grandfather arrive back, happy, but hungry. Paul pours a brandy for his father. Gabriella makes sandwiches. Leo has an urgent question for Dad.

"Dad, can I go fishing with you on Monday?"

Silence.

He has been to fish twice already on the new boat, but only for short one-day trips. Paul felt great to have his son with him and delighted to see he is a natural sea-lover, just like himself. But next week's trip is very different. Four days of swordfishing eighty miles off Malta; the last long trip before the lampuki season opens the following week.

Gabriella holds her breath. Paul fingers his chin.

"It would be too much for you, Leo, and I'd be too busy to look after you."

"But I can look after myself, Dad, and I can help you with the lampuki floats. Please Dad?"

Paul turns to Gabriella.

"What do *you* say, Mummy? Isn't it too much for him?"

Before Mummy's reply, Grandpa interjects.

"I'd like to go down there myself for a little trip. I miss it sometimes. If I went next week I could look after Leo, and both of us could help with the lampuki floats."

There is a brief pause while Paul and Gabriella consider this new development. Their eyes meet with a look that says:

'Well, if Grandpa is going, Leo will be well looked after, and everything should be fine.'

Leo receives the signal, rushes to Grandpa and embraces him with a big hug. Grandpa responds lovingly.

They all smile happily except Dom. He is tucking into tasty sandwiches, oblivious to it all.

***

Monday

It's a sleepy Blugarr Bay that the 'St Agatha' and her little crew leave behind at a chilly two a.m. They have an eighty-mile trip to the rich swordfish grounds, midway between the coast of Tunisia and the island of Sicily. The last swordfishing trip of the season, it will take most of the first day to get there; they will use the time to prepare floats for the lampuki fishing, starting next week.

There is always a sense of optimism among Maltese fishermen at the start of the lampuki season. It comes round once a year, tests century-old skills, pays the bills and contributes to the island's general wellbeing.

Around mid-August, large shoals of lampuki inhabit Maltese waters. Not particularly fond of bright sunshine or extreme heat, they seek shelter under any floating object in the sea. The fishermen kindly oblige by providing hundreds of pipe-framed platforms lined with thick layers of cork or polystyrene. The frames are camouflaged with palm branches, and anchored by heavy concrete blocks. Placed at least seven miles from shore, large shoals are soon huddled happily underneath.

When the fishermen are satisfied with the quantity, they set their nets in a circle, lure out the unsuspecting masses with juicy bait; and pull the purse strings. The pretty little fish soon discover a new home; the dark, icy hold of the trawler. Lampuki are delicious when cooked as only the Maltese can. The main ingredients of many traditional recipes, the fishermen provide them in abundance.

Perched high over the bridge of the 'St Agatha' is a large wire mesh cage designed to store the hundreds of polystyrene floats for use in the lampuki frames. These floats comprise four bricks of polystyrene tied together in a neat parcel.

The crew set to work. Paul puts the boat on automatic pilot and proceeds to organise the assembly line. Mario shapes and groups the polystyrene bricks into squares of four. Ali ties them horizontally and vertically. Leo is high up on the cage receiving the tied blocks from Grandpa and stacking them neatly. Paul provides a constant supply of the component parts. It's an interesting little task, but not a heavy one. They will relax when the scorching sun says it's time to stop.

As the bow of the 'St Agatha slices the blue Mediterranean, Paul is observing with fascination his little team. Three generations of his family, fitting like pieces of Lego into a delightful, working pyramid. What a pity that heartless villain, *old age,* is now to deprive them of a gifted, experienced seaman, who never knew or wanted any other life. He can understand how his father is in his element today on this bonus trip. Five years of living alone has not been easy. The cancer that claimed his loving wife, Maria, also took a large portion of him. The joy of fishing helped him cope. But retirement was an upheaval, replacing contentment and fulfilment with emptiness and boredom. Today, the enjoyment he feels working alongside his grandson, fills him with new energy and enthusiasm. As Leo grows, he can see Dad volunteering for many more trips; providing stimulating therapy for mind and body.

Leo too, is a gift to behold. High up over his crewmates, working assiduously, the picture of happiness and contentment. Paul is now convinced that the magic of the sea has already captured his young heart - from his own youth he knows exactly what joy and exhilaration that can bring. He can now envisage, with optimism and pleasure, many fruitful years of fishing contentment, stretching far into the future. An almost exact replica of the years he and his father worked together except for one important change: the 'St Agatha' has unveiled new horizons. Observing his eleven-year-old son today, so focussed and happy, Paul is more convinced than ever that the decision to incur this massive and risky expenditure was enlightened and correct. Unlike the years of hard slog that he and his father endured, the future for Leo, himself, and hopefully Dom, will be much easier and far more rewarding.

Within two hours of 'destination swordfish' the deck temperature is a sizzling thirty-five degrees. The crew, having stuffed themselves with Gabriella's goodies, are relaxing in the galley before the real work begins in the evening cool.

The Rolling Hitch, the Bowline, the Anchor Bend, the Round Turn and the Half Hitch are just some of the rope knots used on fishing boats. There are many more and Grandpa is showing his grandson how to make them. Of all the lessons Leo has learned at school, this is by far the most interesting. He is determined to master at least a dozen knots before returning home on Friday.

Mario is teaching Ali how to play cards. This basic training course has been conducted during leisure breaks for the past few weeks and due to Ali's sharp learning ability, the teacher is now beginning to loose money to his pupil. They argue and shout, but it's soon forgotten. Paul enjoys the exchanges.

Sailing on autopilot, Paul has time to visit the engine room for some routine inspections. He climbs down and begins the checklist: engine oil, hydraulics, pressure gauges, pumps, batteries, fuel lines, back-up generator. All fine except for one little concern. Added to the usual cocktail of engine room fumes is a strange new odour. Paul tries to identify it and its source. He rechecks everything. It's a mystery. The engine is droning tunefully. No oil leaks on to hot pipes. No exhaust leaks. No acid leaks from the batteries. Perhaps it's just his sensitive nose. He decides to leave it for now and continue to monitor it at short regular intervals.

The 'St. Agatha' is now in the heart of the Mediterranean's best swordfishing grounds, close to the quaint little island of Lampeduca. It's six p.m. on this sultry Monday evening, the sea is barely rippling. As darkness approaches, Paul and his crew get ready for action. Swordfish are not the most endearing of animals. As the name implies, their claim to fame is the sword-like bony extension to their upper jaw. This strong, sharp sword varies in length, but a fully-grown swordfish, weighing up to 100kg, will wield a sword of at least five feet. They are not to be trifled with; angry swordfish have been known to deploy their weapons with devastating effect. During daylight hours, swordfish are in the depths of the ocean hunting for food. Succulent fresh mackerel, cod, squid, hake, bluefish, are gobbled up and savoured. At night as they follow their prey to the surface, they themselves become victims of 'Longliners' like Paul. 'Longliners' get their name from the method of fishing they use, called 'Longlining'. It's a traditional skill of setting a long, horizontal line, with short vertical lines, hooked and baited, attached at thirty feet intervals.

It's as if a long clothesline was set under water with short vertical lines clipped on to hang down, with tasty mackerel or squid hooked on to the ends. But it would need to be a giant clothesline because most fishermen set lines of up to thirty miles. Attached to ball buoys on the surface, longlines float at a depth of about fifty feet.

Every four miles of line a floating aluminium pole is attached. This has a radar-reflecting plate on top that appears clearly on the radar screen, a valuable aid to the skipper. Little radio transmitters are also attached to the line every ten miles, sending a low-frequency signal to the trawler; a help to locate the line at all times.

Paul enters the wheelhouse, happy that his team is ready to start. Each crewmember has a task. His father, looking calm and contented, is in charge of the winch and drum that will feed the line across the deck, via overhead blocks, through a guide ring over the stern and into the water. Mario, his skimpy tee shirt exposing his good looks and strong muscles, is positioned at the stern rail beside a bench and a tub full of freshly thawed mackerel. Ali, his broad smile highlighting his handsome brown face and pearly-white teeth, is to his left with spools of short lines with stainless steel clips on one end, hooks attached to the other. These are called 'Leaders'. Ali's job is to have one ready to place in Mario's hand at half-minute intervals. Mario is such a speed-baiter that he can receive a 'leader', clip it to the moving line, impale the mackerel; deposit the lot into the sea in about twenty seconds. Paul is tuned in to Mario's clockwork baiting; smoothly adjusts the trawler's speed accordingly. Leo has a job too. He is in charge of the ball buoys, handing one to Mario to clip on to the line after every three hooks. It's an efficient little assembly line. Each worker is an important cog in the wheel. Four hours should see the end of the line, and hopefully, the end for lots of big, fat swordfish.

*

"Lord Jesus, protect us from all harm and grant us a good catch of fish. Amen."

It's all quiet and peaceful aboard the 'St. Agatha' as Paul and his young son finish their night prayers before climbing into their bunks. It has been a long day for Leo. Working since dawn, competing with adults all day, a first night away from home, sharing a cabin at sea with his father; he doesn't seem a bit overawed, showing a maturity far beyond his years.

Observing him work so diligently all day, his aptitude and learning capacity, his calm demeanour in new and unfamiliar situations, Paul can see his son becoming a Master Skipper in the future and a little tinge of pride warms his heart.

"Dad, do you pray for fish every time you set the line?"

"Yes, I do. You know when Jesus was on earth he had a special love for fishermen."

"I know."

"Oh! You're well informed, Leo, tell me more."

"Well, I know that when he met the fishermen on the Sea of Galilee, he filled their boat with fish and then made them follow him to a new life."

"That's very good, Leo, you learned that at school?"

"Yes, I always like stories about fishermen."

"Well, now you know why we pray to Jesus for plenty fish."

"Does that mean that fishermen who don't believe in Jesus get no fish?"

"No, it doesn't, Son. They get fish too, maybe *we* get a little more."

"How many will we get in the morning?"

"I don't really know."

"Guess, Dad, give a guess."

"No, it would be tempting fate."

"Ten big ones!"

"I hope you're right, Leo."

"I wonder what's Mummy and Dom doing now?"

"I'd say they are snug in their beds. You should try and sleep now, tomorrow won't be long coming."

Okay, Dad. Good night."

"Good night, Son."

✳✳✳

Tuesday

While his crew sleeps on, Paul rises at four, mounts the bridge and steers the 'St. Agatha' back to the start of the mainline. He is guided by the little radio transmitters, bleeping faintly in the calm ocean. Two hours at full steam and the end bleeper is now at strong volume, almost there. It's time to wake the dreamers.

Around the Mediterranean, dawn is a fast mover. Black darkness becomes blue brightness in the space of fifteen minutes. From slow-motion silhouettes, the crewmembers are now darting around the deck preparing in hopeful anticipation for a rewarding haul-back. Paul is in the engine room checking everything and trying to sniff out the mysterious odour that was bothering him on the trip down from Malta. He can still smell it, but it is not nearly as pungent as it was yesterday; perhaps it will soon be gone altogether.

'Haul-back' is a group operation and must be done with precision and teamwork. It is almost the opposite of 'line setting' except for all the water and slop it dumps on to the deck, making balance and footwork much more hazardous.

Paul will be directing operations from the deck, using the remote helm controls. This allows him to steer the boat, control the engines, operate the hydraulic line spool, all with one hand, leaving his other hand free to 'feel' the line and 'tension' from big juicy 'swingers'.

Fish will be pulled up through an opening in the starboard rail. That's where Mario and Ali are set and ready to welcome them aboard. As the mainline travels from sea to spool, empty 'leaders' will be 'unsnapped' by Mario, 'unbaited' by Ali, passed to Dad, who will coil them, placing them neatly in their drum. Leo is again in charge of the ball buoys. As they arrive on deck he will unsnap them from the mainline, then hang them tidily on a 'clothesline'.

All set and ready, Paul starts the haul-back. This always excites him. His whole working life is geared towards this. He has invested everything to make this moment fruitful. His wife and sons are the motivating force that drives him on. Success feels all the sweeter when he knows his family are the main beneficiaries. Nothing else matters. He feels good today, especially with his father and son sharing the excitement.

The first ten 'leaders' arrive on deck swinging free. Leo's glance towards his dad conveys disappointment.

Paul shouts: "Don't worry boys. The more empty ones come in - the nearer we are to a full one."

He doesn't have long to wait. His 'feel' of the line says tension. As the strain increases, so does his excitement. He has landed many big fish over the years but the thrill never diminishes. He stops the boat, engages reverse gear and slows the line spool. Mario and Ali grab their gaff poles and wait. They watch the steel-tight line climb steadily upwards. It has to be a big one. It is, and alive. Leo is leaning over the rail watching excitedly as the big, blue and purple swordfish slashes madly with its magnificent sword.

Mario and Aly in unison sink their gaff hooks into the fish, steering it to the starboard gate. Paul arrives with his meat hook, joins in the lift and soon a seventy-five kg swordfish adorns the deck.

"Bravo!!!... Big...Lovely...Nice!" exclaims Ali in his broken English.

"What a beauty!" enthuses Mario. "Welcome aboard!"

"Great to get a big one first." says Grandpa.

Leo is speechless. It's the first time he has seen a swordfish being caught. He is thrilled to be part of it. Paul shares his son's delight.

"You enjoyed that, Leo?"

"Sure did, Dad. Our prayers are working."

"Yes, but we must get more like him. Say another little prayer."

"I sure will."

With the fish resting in his icebox in the hold, the happy team continue the haul-back. After six more slack leaders, another visitor arrives - a wonderful specimen of 'fish-hood.' Despite his 100kg weight, he is hauled on board and given a hero's welcome. He doesn't appreciate the experience, is in no mood to conform. His audience enjoy the show as he dances and bobs around the sloppy deck, stubbornly refusing to surrender.

Bravely, he continues to jump and bounce, exhausting his fast-diminishing energy. But now his strength is failing, his eyes are losing their sparkle, his rich, purple blue sheen is fading to a dull grey. Defeated, he will soon rest peacefully in the cool darkness beside his mate.

The crewmembers are jubilant. Excitement and anticipation is filling them with new strength and energy. But trawler life can be a roller coaster. Paul is well used to flying starts that fizzle out. He will not get carried away. Grandpa too, is experienced in the fickle ways of the sea. That's where Paul learned calmness and awareness, and the ability to accept with gratitude, whatever harvest the sea delivers on to your deck.

The 'St. Agatha' is now abreast of the second beeper, which means the crew has hauled back one hundred 'leaders'. It's been a great morning. The number of sleeping beauties in the hold have now risen to five. The first of the three sections has now been hauled back. It has taken two hours and produced about 300kg. of quality swordfish. Paul figures that at this rate, cautiously assuming a similar catch, it will be well into the afternoon before they are finished.

Grandpa heads for the galley. Leo is delighted. Landing big swordfish is hungry work. He would like to help Grandpa with the cooking but has to stay at his important post on deck. Soon the crew will be savouring big bowls of pot noodles, basking in the success of their morning's work.

With full bellies, nicely refreshed, the crew resume the haul-back. It's mid-morning, the sun is getting really hot. The two 'gaffers' have peeled off their morning wrappings, Mario, showing off his black, hairy chest, Ali, his youthful, chocolate curves and velvet soft features. Grandpa and Leo have also stripped off. The little team are ready to receive their next visitor.

He soon arrives. Paul feels serious tension on the line. This is a monster. Slowly, carefully, the mainline, vibrating with strain, is winched up. The fish, a real giant, hits the surface. Ali and Mario cheer in unison. Grandpa and Leo watch in amazement. Paul is apprehensive. This fellow is huge. It's going to be a real battle. The fish jumps and dives. Paul gives him more line, waits for him to relax, pulls again. For half an hour the ritual is repeated. The strength of three fit men is not enough to force the warrior from the sea. Paul tells Mario and Ali to ease off and perhaps the fish will relax again. The monster has no intention of obliging. His strength and energy seems to increase. He wants to dive to the depths. Paul wants to keep him on the surface. Unable to physically hold him with their tired arms, the men are forced to use the starboard rail to hold the line and anchor him. They hope to steer him to the proximity of the gaff hooks. This is exactly what the 'Joker' is waiting for. With a mighty leap and a corkscrew twist, he breaks the line just above the hook, dives to freedom and his victory lap to the deep. The villain is gone.

A huge wave of disappointing anti-climax envelops the crew. After such an exhilarating morning this was to be the icing on the cake. Paul is bitterly disappointed. He joins the deflated group still staring at the spot where their 'prize-fighter' entered the water and absconded. Mario straightens up, exasperation flushing his face.

"The one that got away …why is it always the biggest one?"

Pained expressions on the faces of the others signal agreement, but without an answer.

"Never mind boys." Paul tries to lift them again, "our best wasn't good enough. We met more than our match. Fair play to him. But there are lots more where he came from. Come-on, let's go and bring them in."

The gloom doesn't last long. The second and third sections were hectic. Under a scorching sun the little crew sweated through four hours of exhausting toil. Tiredness or aching limbs didn't bother them. It was a labour of love. Seven big ones in the second section and nine in the third calculate to twenty-one big juicy swordfish resting on ice beds in the hold. It was really hard work but no one is complaining. Paul is delighted. Grandpa gives all the credit to Leo who is brimming with joy and excitement.

*

It's mid-afternoon, the day's work is only half done. The 'St Agatha' must turn 180 degrees, sail back thirty miles to begin setting out for to-morrow's catch.

After a shower, a change of clothes and a hearty meal, the men relax in the galley. Paul is in the engine room for his routine checks. Everything seems in order except for the strange smell;

it's still there. It seems to be stronger today, with a definite sniff of gas. It's a mystery to Paul. He calls his father for his opinion. He is puzzled too. They recheck everything; still no evidence of its source. Wafting around, almost visible, yet they can't identify it.

"What do think, Dad?"

"I haven't a clue, Paul. It's not an oil smell, an exhaust smell or a fuel smell. It's a complete mystery."

"I know, I'll have to have it checked and fixed the minute we get home."

As Paul steers the 'St Agatha' back along the fertile trail to his setting-out start point, he reflects on the day's brilliant catch. For future reference he tries to analyse the factors that contributed to it. The first important point is that he had found a strip of extra warm water, flanked by a cooler stream. This is a haven for schools of plankton, mackerel and squid. Swordfish are in their element trashing through shoals. It's their banquet and they feast in thousands.

Paul will use the same rich strip for his remaining two sets, hoping the multitudes are still feasting. Another factor that favoured Paul was the absence of other trawlers from his lucky grounds. He hasn't seen one all day. Many of them are tied up preparing lampuki frames for next week's opening. Others are fishing close to home, returning every night. Paul doesn't feel lonely – lots of big fat swordfish are good company.

Down in the galley a lively game of cards is underway. Mario's luck is in today - Ali's money is getting scarce. He doesn't worry too much. He is only lending it to Mario; to be returned to-morrow. Anyway, if today's catch is repeated over the next two days, he will be receiving a big fat share at the weekend.

Grandpa and Leo are again surrounded by a selection of ropes.

"Will you show me some new ones to-day, Grandpa?"

Leo has mastered all the main knots but is determined to learn many more.

"Okay, Leo, three more."

Grandpa is impressed. He remembers when Paul was Leo's age, he had the same urge to learn. Everything about the sea and fishing interested him. His mind recorded and retained every snippet of information that came his way. To be a successful fisherman was his only vocation in life. It was easy to see him becoming a fine skipper, which he is. He can now see Leo following in his father's footsteps. That thought warms his heart.

The signal is given by Paul to start the second setting. Mario and Ali lift the transmitter buoy over the stern, lowering it into the sea behind the boat. The mainline, attached to the beeper, starts to roll off the winch spool into the water. The little assembly line is now in motion. Paul synchronises the boat speed; guides it along the warm, fertile strip. Grandpa controls the winch spool. 'Leaders' are baited and snapped on to the mainline by Mario and Ali. Ball buoys click into place from Leo's clockwork timing. It will take four hours of steady work. The cosy little bunks below water level will nestle tired bodies tonight.

Wednesday

The 'St. Agatha' purrs through the smooth sea as the stars twinkle and the pale moon floats gracefully over the lingering clouds. Guided by the little transmitter buoys, she hugs the mainline back thirty miles to its starting point. Paul is the epitome of contentment, high on the bridge, eagerly anticipating another rewarding haulback. It's 5 a.m. and while his workforce remain cuddled up in a deep, muscle soothing sleep, he has time to admire and savour the tranquil beauty of early morning in the peaceful Mediterranean. He chuckles to himself as he glances over the rippling water, shimmering under a pearly grey dome. He knows that his enjoyment of the surroundings is linked to yesterday's excellent fishing. A generous sea that yields up lots of prize swordfish is always beautiful. Hopefully to-morrow, he will feel the same affection for this big, friendly ocean.

The sleeping beauties nestling in their bunks just below the waterline are centre stage in Paul's reflective thoughts. They are all heroes. Yesterday's 12 hours of hard labour in the sweltering heat was some brave effort. Aching limbs, tired eyes and energy-drained bodies, didn't prompt protest or complaint. For them it was a labour of love. Exhausted, but happy, they fell into their bunks.

Paul would dearly love to have his father and son on every trip. It feels so right. Three generations of a family of sea lovers working and sharing as one, harvesting the rich fruit of the ocean, doing the thing they love to do, fulfilled with contentment and happiness. Sadly, Dad will have to opt out. What a pity old age is such a spoilsport. Leo will take his place. This week proves what a great fisherman he will make in the years ahead.

Restored by six hours of deep sleep, energised by a nourishing breakfast, infused with enthusiasm for another day of excitement, the crewmembers are on deck, ready for the haulback. Paul has completed his work in the engine room. Everything seems fine, all readings as they should be, all gauges reporting correctly, the big engine droning sweetly. The only concern is the villain of a smell, still persisting, and will not identify itself. Not his sensitive nose or his imagination, it is a real, foul odour. It is annoying him because it won't reveal its source.

Paul is now positioned at the deck helm station where he will control and direct the haulback with the remote controls. To activate the system, the autopilot is turned to the 'remote' setting, allowing him to operate the engine controls, the steering and the hydraulic mainline spool. He can do all this with one hand, leaving the other free to 'feel' tension on the incoming mainline, signalling the presence of a big, blue/purple visitor complete with sword.

Mario and Ali are at the starboard rail ready to usher the visitor onboard using their long gaff poles. Grandpa will also assist a reluctant visitor on to the deck with a 24-inch steel meat hook. Not a very dignified entrance for such a noble aristocrat, but Paul and his crew are satisfied 'the end justifies the means'

Leo is again in charge of the incoming ball buoys. Receiving and storing them neatly is an important task in the smoothly running assembly line. By now he has the work so refined, it's no longer a challenge. Soon it will even become boring. He would welcome a promotion.

The haulback begins with the important task of retrieving the transmitter buoy from the water and securing it safely on deck. Mario guides it up and, helped by Ali, lifts it over the railing. It is switched off, unclipped from the mainline and stowed away. The line is then fed through the blocks on to the winch spool, the slack is rolled up to a nice even tension as it enters the water at an angle of about 30 degrees.

The boat in gear, the throttle and spool speed synchronised, Paul steers a course parallel to the mainline as Mario and Ali unclip the leaders emerging from the water. The first few are slack, no fish; no concern. It's early days, the men are busy unclipping the leaders, unhooking the bait fish, dumping them into the sea.

Paul feels extra tension on the line as it slides through his hand. He feels an extra little bit of excitement too as the line tightens and the angle sharpens. He lowers the throttle, knocks the engine out of gear while closely monitoring the tight mainline as it slowly rolls on to the winch pool. Three men are now leaning over the rail waiting to receive their guest. Grandpa in the centre is guiding the line up to the surface while Mario and Ali are poised with their gaffs. Leo is an excited spectator ready to assist if he is needed. The fish comes into view, pulses begin to race, eyes widen, and smiles adorn faces. He is big, strong and beautiful. He thrashes and circles, tries to seek refuge under the boat, but despite his reluctance, he is forced to conform. Using patience and waiting tactics, Grandpa manoeuvres him close enough for the 'gaffers' to act. In perfect unison Mario and Ali sink the gaff hooks into his head. Paul's 24-inch meat hook completes the execution. All hands are now required to heave the flailing, slippery missile on to the deck, where he continues to buck and bounce. The show is over when the main attraction runs out of energy, eventually out of life. A 100kg sword landed, is a triumph for the crew and a great start to the day.

A series of slack leaders arriving with nothing but bait fish attached, brings the euphoria on deck back to zero, but the crew are busy; the haulback is proceeding like clockwork. The hot morning sun prompts a peeling off of excess clothing. Paul and his team are nicely cool now.

Two mini-swords arrive in quick succession. The first, only a baby, is unhooked; sent diving back into the sea. The second, about 15kg, is not so lucky. He is taken aboard to join his peers in the icy hold.

Paul is always mindful of the necessity for responsible fish conservation. He knows that over-fishing is endangering many species. In recent years the average size of swordfish being caught is reducing alarmingly. They are not being allowed to grow to maturity. This annoys Paul. He will always release the small ones, especially those that are not injured and sure to survive.

Nearly all of the first section of mainline is now hauled back, yielding six fish of various sizes. Paul estimates their average weight to be about 40kg each, making a total of 240kg, a good morning's work.

The second beeper is hauled aboard, followed by two big swordfish. Euphoria is again filling the deck. The heat is oppressive; there are no complaints, all are happy. This second section is even better than the first. From fifty leaders to halfway, another five swords are taken. It's heavy work in the sweltering heat. Arms aching, sweat pouring, fatigue is great, but the reward is greater.

The absence of fish from about twenty leaders gives the crew a little respite. It's only temporary, soon they are again under severe pressure. The excitement welling up in Paul is sparked off by the absence from the surface of several ball buoys, dragged to the depths by something really big and heavy. The severe tension on the mainline confirms it. If this is a fish, he must be a giant. Could it be possible that another monster had made the mistake of taking the bait? It would be a bit incredulous to suggest that yesterday's massive joker had guilty feelings, came back to surrender.

Yes! It's a fish. Paul and his wide-eyed, excited crew can't see him yet – he is rolling, diving and pulling like a tug-of-war team, twenty fathoms down – but all are agreed on one thing, he is gigantic. They agree on something else; this fellow is not getting away; is coming aboard. Slowly and carefully the mainline is eased up on the hydraulic spool. Paul will give this fellow plenty of time to expend his hyper exuberance.

For an hour, the game of 'snakes and ladders' is played. Each glimpse of the bright surface seems to be the catalyst that triggers a massive lunge and dive to the deep, undoing the patient, energy-sapping efforts of Paul and his crew. Yesterday's mistake will not be repeated. The mainline will not be locked. He can have as many dives as it takes to tire and frustrate him. A prize like him is worth waiting for. All he wants is a locked line, to allow him wrestle this painful, steel tooth from his mouth. Paul is the dentist, will not oblige.

The monster fish eventually breaks the surface, showing his massive proportions. This fellow is even bigger than the one that got away yesterday. The astonished crew foolishly thinks the fight is over; the fish has other ideas. He just wants to see and assess the enemy. His curiosity satisfied, one mighty plunge takes him ten fathoms under, out of sight, but not yet out of danger. Paul still has him hooked.

For another half an hour the crew, with aching arms, shoulders and legs, fight the giant until he again emerges, tired, exasperated. Paul and his father join forces, trying to drag him towards the hull. Mario and Ali are ready with the gaffs. Leo is exhilarated with the excitement of it all.

Now almost on 'death row' with his executioners sensing victory, the massive fish suddenly realises his predicament, decides he is not yet ready to concede. With one mighty slap of his tail, he rolls, twists, dives ten fathoms into the deep, leaving the shocked crew speechless, and forced to start all over again.

Paul is determined not to loose this fish. It is the biggest swordfish he has ever seen. He still has him on the leader. He will do nothing to facilitate the extraction of his steel tooth. There is no hurry. If the hook is strong enough, so is he. Slowly and smoothly he lures him again to the surface, his endurance is failing; it is time for an all out effort to get him close. Eight tired, but committed arms are too strong for the twisting, thrashing brute. Paul and his father hold him close enough for Mario and Ali to sink their gaff hooks deep into his proud head. The 'gaffers' hold him while two big meat hooks are added to his jewellery. After a mighty heave, he is doing his dance of death around the sloppy deck. Mario and Ali are dancing too, an exotic belly dance in tempo with the bobbing, twisting fish.

This is a monster. As his strength ebbs away and he approaches the end of what must have been a long life, Paul and his team of exhausted champions bask in the glory of their fantastic victory. It is a chance of a lifetime to catch such a prize specimen, an even greater achievement to fight a fierce battle, win the war, and bring him on board.

After a further eight swordfish of various sizes are hauled aboard, the end of the 'golden' mainline is reached. The exhausted crew hose the slush from the deck, tidy the equipment, before staggering below to change their sweaty clothes. A soothing shower, a good nourishing meal and a deserved rest leaves the crew relaxed and happy as they relive a memorable day's fishing. Twenty lovely corpses added to yesterday's twenty-one is some haul. If tomorrow's catch is anyway similar, they will be heading for Bluegarr with a day to spare.

Paul rings Gabriella on the satellite phone. She is thrilled to hear news of the great fishing, 41 big juicy swords in only two days. She is even more delighted when Paul says he will probably be home a day earlier if to-morrow's catch is as good.

Gabriella is really missing Leo. She urgently needs news of his wellbeing. Paul puts her mind at ease. He is full of praise of their son's ability and maturity. Proudly he expresses his delight at Leo's excellent behaviour, his natural aptitude for fishing. He also conveys his joy at seeing his father, Leo and himself working so well as a team of three generations. Gabriella shares Paul's pleasure but cautions him against allowing their eleven-year-old to become too pre-occupied with fishing and the sea, to the detriment of his school education. Paul's own schooldays finished when he was thirteen, Grandpa's at twelve. They both became successful fishermen. He now agrees with Gabriella that their two sons will have a proper formal education. They realise that fishing, with today's science and technology, requires ability and education as never before. Leo arrives on the bridge at an opportune moment. Paul says goodbye to Gabriella, hands the phone to Leo.

"Mummy wants to talk to you."

"Hi Mummy … this is great …I'm a real fisherman now …I can set the ball buoys …I can stack the lampuki floats …I can make all the fishermen's knots …I can cook with Grandpa in the galley …you should see the size of the swordfish."

"Hold on Leo …take your time. I know you are enjoying yourself. But you mustn't get too excited. Have you thought about Dom and me? Do you miss me at all?"

"Course I do Mummy …But I have Dad and Grandpa …Tell Dom I have lots of things to tell him when I come home."

"Are you saying your prayers every day? I told you that you must not forget Holy God."

"No Mummy, I didn't forget. Me and Dad pray every night for a good catch."

"That's good, Leo, but there's lots of other things to pray for besides fish."

"I know, Mummy, but the more I pray for fish, the more fish we get …God loves fishermen …Even Dad knows that …He always prays for fish."

"All right, Leo, but say a little prayer for me and Dom too."

"I will, Mummy, I'll see you when we get home."

"Okay, Love, mind yourself; I really miss you. Bye Love."

Thursday

It's mid-day. The third haulback is completed. The arms of every crewmember ached. Their heavy eyes were stinging and their empty bellies rumbled. But when Paul said, "It's time to hit for home" his words were met with smiling faces and relieved hearts; the minor ailments forgotten about. The morning's catch added twenty-three more big swords to the forty-one already adorning the icy hold. Paul was tempted to continue for another set. This fertile strip is a rare discovery. 'We may not find one as rich again.' He is full of gratitude to God. But he must not be greedy. Sixty-four big fish in three hauls is brilliant. His crew has proved to be a great little team.

To have his father and son aboard makes it even more special. Yes, it's time to steam for Bluegarr Bay and share all this happiness with Gabriella and Dom. He can't wait to hug and kiss them.

Grandpa and Leo are busy in the galley cooking. It's a really cool novelty for Leo. He loves pot noodles and Grandpa is an expert. Mario and Ali are changing from their sloppy work clothes, washing and shaping up for the return home. They'll appear in the galley soon, ravenous for grub. Paul is doing his engine room checks for the six hour journey home. The smell is stronger today, still no evidence as to its origin. He double-checks everything. The battery cases are a bit warmer than usual. He wonders if they are over charging. That might be it. There is a hint of acid in the smell. He will get an engineer to thoroughly check everything to-morrow.

The crew have all eaten; it's time to steam back to Malta. Three nights of great fishing means a day earlier home. It's a lovely feeling of satisfaction and contentment. Paul is happy at the helm as he accelerates, leaving a trail of churning white foam in his wake. Mario and Ali are dealing the cards. This session will be the decider. Ali feels lucky. Both are now certain of a brilliant pay packet; already mentally planning a little spending spree.

Grandpa and Leo are cleaning and tidying the galley before

returning to the rope knots for a final refresher course. Leo has kept a little diary of his trip. The knots already mastered are listed. He wants to learn more. He has also documented the catch from each line set. In their bunks at night, chatting before falling asleep, He challenged his dad to guess the weight of the day's catch. Based on that estimate he has recorded a total haul of 2000 kg of swordfish. He is really looking forward to seeing the real, official weight. He can then check and confirm the true extent of his dad's brilliance.

It's mid-afternoon, the St. Agatha is slicing through the blue Mediterranean with a smooth swish, in harmony with the drone of her powerful engine. Halfway home, Paul engages the automatic pilot, leaves the wheelhouse, goes to the galley and helps himself to a mug of strong coffee. That freshens him up with a spurt of new energy. He says he is going to the bow to tidy up the little heap of assorted floats there. These are mainly empty plastic water bottles and detergent containers. They are normally stored in the overhead frame but were moved to accommodate the lampuki floats. Leo says he wants to help. Grandpa will prepare the evening meal. Mario and Ali have gone to their bunks for a short sleep. They will need all their energy when they reach the harbour for the unloading of almost two tonnes of fish. Paul returns to the bridge to check the auto pilot settings. Happy that they are steaming a straight path to Bluegarr, he joins Leo in the bow. An old square of net comes in handy for what they have to do. Spreading it out, they pile the empty plastic containers on to it. Gathering up the edges to form a purse, they tie it tightly, then fasten it safely to the deck rail to make sure it doesn't blow overboard. Job done, they smile and admire their handiwork.

Leo joins Grandpa in the galley. Paul is heading back to the bridge. Passing the stairs that leads down to the engine room, he is knocked back by a suffocating smell.

"Jesus, Christ Almighty!" A bolt of terror hits him.

The fumes are so intense he has to grab his nose and mouth to avoid choking.

He desperately tries to force his way down. He can't. He needs something … breathing apparatus …a mask …anything to allow him to breathe.

He shouts for help. Grandpa and Leo run from the galley. Shocked, they watch Paul battling against the thick fumes, coughing, choking, descending; retreating.

"Quick" he shouts, "get me something …anything … quick … to cover my face."

They both turn. Leo runs, is back in seconds with a large white towel. Paul grabs it, wraps it around his face. He forces his way down. About to enter, a blast of gas lifts him off his feet, hurls him back on the steps. Sprawling, disorientated, he struggles to his feet.

He tries again. Another massive gust of fumes and gas lands him again on his back. Like a switched-on furnace, the whole engine room suddenly ignites in a huge blast of fire. The doorway is a blowtorch. Flames gush everywhere. Tongues of fire spurt out, up the stairs, over him, licking his body. He can smell his hair burning, his neck and arms scorching. He manages to clamber up, step by step, singed and stunned. His father grabs him, desperately pulling him up.

Paul shouts for the others. Leo runs down, bangs on their cabin door, screaming. They jump out, run to the deck, half-naked. "Water," roars Paul, "get the hose, quick." They run. Paul, shaken, half-blind, straightens up. "Fire extinguisher!" He shouts to Mario: "In the wheelhouse ...quick!"

The fire is now raging wild. Paul tells his father to take Leo to the bow and shield him there. Mario frantically sprays water at full power. Paul descends the steps with the fire extinguisher. He is forced to stop halfway down. He trains the extinguisher hose on the doorway, about to pull the lever. BANG! BANG! A thunderous explosion blasts him against the steps.

The extinguisher imprints his chest. He winces in pain, drops it, crawls back up on hands and knees. Mario and Ali pull him clear. The fire is out of control. They are forced back. Mario continues to spray. It's useless.

"Keep spraying! Keep spraying! Jesus! Keep spraying!" Paul is distraught.

BANG! BANG! BANG! Another massive explosion rips through the whole centre of the boat. Rocking, rolling and vibrating violently, she erupts in a raging furnace. Splinters and fragments of fireballs penetrate the sky, disintegrate, and rain down like fireworks.

The wheelhouse is wrecked, shattered and burning. The engine is silent, its drone replaced by the roar of flames and blazing fibreglass.

Paul is flung against the starboard railing, blinded, winded, punch-drunk. His shirt is ripped into rags, his jeans tattered and torn to shreds.

Mario is catapulted into the air, landing in a heap of concussion on the deck. Gasping and groaning, writhing in agony, his right shoulder badly injured.

Ali is blasted like a missile towards the bow. He lands, head first, on the steel deck, tumbles over, lies motionless, knocked out.

Grandpa is sent staggering against the bow, hitting the steel rail with a bruising blow of his head. Blood flows down the back of his neck. He still manages to hold on to Leo, cushioning his fall. Leo isn't hurt but is now screaming with anguish for his prostrated dad. With head throbbing, vision hazy, Grandpa struggles across the deck to assist his stricken son. Leo, in terror, follows him. "No," shouts Grandpa, "stay where you are ...you'll be burned."

Paul is moaning, unable to breathe, holding his chest. His father lifts him to a sitting position. His eyes have a haunting, tortured stare. He opens his mouth to speak. Nothing comes out. He is still winded. Grandpa removes the towel from around his neck, placing it under his head as he eases him back to a lying position. Paul is having none of it. Despite the intense pain of a bruised chest and cracked ribs, he is determined to get up.

Flames are raging violently. Showers of sparks are raining down everywhere. He has to move ...fast. Gripping the rail with one hand, he offers the other to his father. It's an excruciating effort but he makes it. Holding his ribs with one hand, his father with the other, he shuffles towards the bow. Bent over the rail he waits to regain his breath. Placing a hand on Leo's shoulder to reassure him, he whispers hoarsely "Grandpa will look after you ...we'll be alright."

He shuffles over to Mario, helps him to his feet. He is groggy, has double vision and moaning with the pain of his shoulder. His collarbone seems to be broken.

Grandpa helps Ali up. Dazed and dizzy, his head is bleeding; he is badly disorientated. He can't stand, keeps staggering backwards, he has to sit again.

The fire is now a raging inferno. The whole of the mid-ship is ablaze. Paul is dazed and devastated. They are all shocked, shaken and terrorised. But Paul is the skipper. He must do something. He turns in desperation to his father, now shielding his trembling grandson from the intensifying heat.

"What can we do?" What will we do? We have to get help. We can't send out a 'Mayday'. The bridge is gone. Jesus Christ, what will we do?" He is shouting.

"The life raft." We have to get it in the water," screams Grandpa, his mind confused, and his head 'splitting'. He can't think straight.

"But we can't get it. How can we get it? The fire won't let us go to the stern where everything is."

"Can someone swim to it?"

"But who can? Mario is the only swimmer. He has concussion and a broken shoulder. Leo is the only other swimmer. Oh, Christ, what will we do?"

Paul tries desperately to think of something. He knows the reality of their catastrophic situation. The boat is lost, destroyed, wrecked. It's now a life saving task.

He realises the awful truth that all the instruments and equipment for sending a 'Mayday' are on the bridge, incinerating into ashes at this very moment. He is also now painfully aware that all their lifesaving equipment is in the stern, completely unreachable through the 'Gates of Hell' that is now the mid-ship. They have no life jackets, no inflatable life raft, no flares, no radar, no radio, nothing to elert anyone to their calamitous situation. No means of sending a distress signal. Not even his mobile phone; it's on the bridge.

Paul spots one glimmer of hope. It is hanging from the deck rail where he and Leo tied it: the net bag of empty containers and floats.

"The net," he exclaims. "Thanks be to Jesus." Untying it from the rail, it looks a flimsy construction on which five lives will have to depend. It's all they have got.

The fire is spreading rapidly. The bridge and all the centre is gone, leaving a black, smouldering, gaping hole. The flames are relentlessly creeping towards both ends. The crew, now huddled in terror at the bow, realises the agonising choice that faces them; **take to the water or burn to death.** Leo is numbed with terror. Grandpa is tenderly holding him, shielding him from the scorching heat that is intensifying with every minute.

Mario is in agony. His shoulder is throbbing, his arm is locked in pain. Paul makes a neck sling from a short piece of light rope, fits it on, giving support and relief to his now swollen arm.

Ali is in terror. He has regained his balance but is still dazed and distraught. A huge red lump has mushroomed through his black curly hair. He keeps crying, praying, asking Paul if they will die. Paul tries to console him and the others.

Out of breath and with difficulty bending, Paul gets to work on the 'net-bag'. Though in terrible pain, Mario tries to help. They hurriedly reform the bag into a more flat shape. With bits of rope they attach more blocks of jablo to strengthen the corners. Now for the painful task of launching. Grandpa and Ali try to help. They manage to lift it over the rail and lower it gently into the sea. The water is calm and blue, except for the shower of firework sparks and frightening red reflection of the blazing trawler. Paul and Mario, with pieces of light rope, try to hold the 'raft' steady, close to the hull. Another short length of rope is tied firmly to the deck rail. It will be the crew's last physical contact with their grief-stricken sea-home as they grip it to slide down the short but perilous descent to the sea.

Grandpa is first to slowly ease himself down. Fully clothed with heavy rubber boots, he wraps his lean hands tightly around the rope. Trembling and gasping and exclaiming "Jesus, Mary and Joseph" he enters the water. Grabbing the 'raft' with both hands, he awkwardly secures his floating position.

Little Leo, without hesitation, bravely slides down the rope.

"Easy, easy, Leo; be careful," Paul slowly helps him down.

Grandpa helps him to lie on top of the net. He is agile and now unbelievably calm.

Distraught, terror-stricken, Ali can't face the ordeal.

"Me no swim …no swim …I die …I die! …no … no!"

It takes all of Paul's persuasive powers to get him down the treacherous slide. Mario has to precede him, holding him as he screams and wails his way down. The sensation of being fully immersed in the sea adds more volume to his screams as he thrashes around, desperately clinging on to Mario and the 'raft' for dear life.

It's now the agonising moment of truth for Paul. He has to go and leave his life's proud possession, wrecked, blazing into oblivion. His last sweeping look is a torturous wrench, seeing his pride and joy dying a cruel death, soon to be buried in the depths of the Mediterranean. His body is blistering from the intensifying furnace, his ribs are broken, his heart is breaking too, but his focus now turns to the massive burden of saving the lives of his precious crew.

He surveys the tragic scene below him. Three injured and terrified men, including his elderly father, floating in a circle around their little makeshift net-table, his young son, bewildered, but courageously perched on top. A sword of grief pierces his heart as he reluctantly grips the rope, abandons his cherished craft; slides down.

As the water envelops him, a shivering of terror almost paralyses his mind and body. He quickly controls himself, knowing that he cannot allow fear or weakness divert his focus from the awesome responsibility of saving his family and crew. Despite the unknown perils that lie ahead, he is determined to protect them, and somehow, organise their safe journey home.

As the traumatised crew and their devastated skipper cling to their flimsy life-bed, they drift slowly away from the blazing wreck. There is hardly a ripple in the sea, the hot sun is beaming down; the water is calm. They have no propulsion, no steering, just the gentle tide to ease them away from the sparks and heat of the raging inferno. The little bag of floats is just about sufficiently buoyant to keep them above water. Fear and apprehension render the little group quiet and subdued, except for Ali. Wailing and screaming, praying and crying, he is inconsolable, despite Paul's pleading.

Grandpa, gasping, is desperately trying to keep his head above water. After a lifetime at sea he still can't swim. Paul ties pieces of polystyrene to his arms to help him float.

Mario is a rock of courage and strength. A strong swimmer, he is now almost paralysed with his broken shoulder. He still manages to float around the 'raft' making sure all are safe.

Paul ties his waist with rope to the net, leaving his hands free to hold Leo, balanced bravely on top. He considers the prospects of their rescue. His anxious eyes sweep around the vast expanse of the Mediterranean for potential rescuers. Only clear blue sky and glistening water can be seen. His ribs are hurting, he has difficulty speaking, but he tries to explain the situation to his crew. They listen attentively, praying for some hope from their skipper to deliver them from this awful plight of doom and disaster.

"We may be rescued before darkness," he declares confidently. "The VMS is our main hope. They will see that it has gone dead. They will then check our last recorded position. When they try to contact us and find everything is dead they will send out 'Search and Rescue' to our position. They have planes, helicopters and fast patrol boats. We could be home before night."

All boats over a certain size have a Vessel Monitoring System (VMS) aboard. This transmits by satellite, the boat's exact position every two hours. It is monitored in the Malta Fisheries Department and is also received by the Armed Forces of Malta. The system is a vital aid to both authorities. The Fisheries Department enforce strict fish conservation and control. The VMS tells them if a boat is fishing in illegal waters. They quickly arrive on the scene and take action.

The Armed Forces use the VMS to monitor and patrol the sea around Malta. Vital services such as search and rescue, fisheries protection, border control, illegal migration, anti-smuggling and maritime surveillance, all depend on the valuable assistance of the VMS.

Although Paul tries his best to convey hope and optimism to his depressed crew, he is tormented with the thought that they haven't a morsel of food or a drop of water to sustain them if their rescue is unduly delayed. He is in dread of a long night of this hardship. Mario is strong and resilient, despite his suffering. Leo, although terrified, is showing great courage. Grandpa is holding up well, but for how long? At his age this suffering must be terrible. Ali is now silent but his eyes are full of terror and awash with tears. Paul shouts an urgent request:

"Nobody drink a drop of seawater. It will kill you!"

Daylight is fading fast over the still waters of the Mediterranean. The orange-like sun sinks gently out of sight. Hope is sinking too from the troubled hearts and minds of the little group.

Having drifted a mile from their ill-fated trawler they can now see her listing severely and about to capsize at any moment. The flames, though not leaping as high as earlier, are still enveloping the fibreglass hull, spreading shimmering red reflections over the darkening sea.

Paul's mind is a furnace too. The searing pain of seeing this beautiful vessel, his pride and joy, his hopes and dreams, now dying this despicable death is breaking his heart. He can hardly watch but is forced to witness the sad, final act of obliteration.

Now lying on her side, the trawler's stern disappears below water as her bow protrudes into the air. As she sinks, the flames are extinguished. It is a slow, agonising death, prolonging the pain of her grief-stricken crew.

Suddenly, the sea opens like a vast mouth. The men watch in horror as the 'St. Agatha', their beautiful craft, the admiration of Bluegarr Bay, is gulped and swallowed into the bowels of the Mediterranean. The flames are extinguished as joint layers of disturbed water fold over the boiling trough. Waves of oily foam belch out in circles from the now closed grave. Within seconds all is calm again and the 'St. Agatha' is in her new home on the bed of the ocean.

As the distraught crew scan the forlorn scene once more, their vision is filled with nothing but a frightening expanse of dismal grey water and their hopes of survival disappearing into the eerie darkness.

Paul's confidence is dealt a shattering blow and much of his optimism is now buried with his beloved boat. He knows that whatever chance the rescue teams had of locating a vessel, especially one on fire, is now gone. There is nothing to attract attention. Their tiny 'raft', without a light or a flare, is a mere speck in the vast ocean. As night envelops the hapless group, the bleakness of isolation fills them with anguish and despair.

*

It's half-seven. Gabreilla is wondering if Paul, Grandpa and Leo will be home soon. Paul said last night on the satellite phone that with a good catch again today, he would head for home and should be in port around six. It would take about an hour to unload; they should be home between seven and eight.

She has been busy all evening preparing a special little treat for the 'fishermen' after their exhausting trip. She knows the hard labour that went into their four days of constant fishing. Leo must be exhausted. Little Dom can't wait to see him and hear all about it. Poor Grandpa must be tired too. He wouldn't be able now for hard punishing work. He'll need a good rest. Being home a day earlier will give them all a long weekend to recover.

A succulent roast chicken is ready and waiting in the oven. With steaming carrots, cauliflower, creamed potatoes, and cheese sauce; it's Paul's favourite dish. Ice cream and fresh fruit salad is ready and waiting to thrill Leo. To-night's little banquet will be extra special with the surprise popping of a big bottle of vintage champagne which she has been saving for the right moment and chilling all afternoon. What better occasion to celebrate than the ending of their first season of great swordfishing and the start of the lampuki season?

*

With the blanket of haze and darkness now covering the Mediterranean, air and water temperature has plummeted to painful levels. Morale among the little freezing group is sinking with every shivering minute. Even Mario, hitherto a rock of calm and courage, is losing his nerve and spirit. He keeps saying to Paul that they will never be found now and will all die of starvation, thirst and exposure. This growing despair from Mario is a serious blow to Paul's confidence, eroding his valiant efforts to keep hope alive.

Ali is crying loudly again, keening, wailing and praying for someone to save him. Grandpa is subdued and peaceful. His forbearance in such terrible conditions impresses Paul. The bitter cold water must be really hurting him. How long can a man of his age survive this?

Leo is being cradled tenderly by his dad. He is brave and courageous, but is now trembling from the bitter cold. With great pain and difficulty, Mario removes his jacket, passes it to Paul, who wraps it round his little shivering son. Paul is touched by Mario's kind gesture, 'a heart of gold in a sea of woe.'

Paul begins the Rosary to Our Lady of Sorrows.

"Incline unto our aid, oh God."

"Oh Lord make haste to help us."

The opening words are a heartfelt plea to the Savour that can deliver them from this watery wilderness. All respond fervently except Ali who keeps crying and chanting his own Islamic prayers. Paul has great faith and always finds solace and favour in his devotion to Our Lady of Sorrows. Many times when in difficulty, she has helped him out. Surely, he reasons, she must come to his aid now in this terrible struggle for survival.

*

Almost ten o'clock and Gabriella has given up all hope of Paul, Grandpa and Leo coming home to-night. She tries for the third time to ring Paul's mobile phone. All she is getting is a jingle that says he is out of range. She tries the satellite phone, but it just gives an 'engaged' tone. She tells Dom to go to bed. His dad won't be home tonight. They must have stayed for another setting.

Trying to make sense of this, she thinks back to Paul's exact words. He didn't say for definite that he would return after this morning's haulback. What he said was that if, as he expected, the catch was good, they would leave it at that, and come home. That leaves only one explanation: the catch must have been bad and he decided to have another setting.

That scenario is almost plausible, but she is still not convinced. It doesn't feel right. Paul would always tell her whether he is coming home or not. He never leaves her guessing and wondering. It isn't like him. He always phones to let her know one way or the other.

Silently, she prays that her worry is unfounded. She feels guilty to be jumping to conclusions at every little change from what would be the norm. But she is always aware of the dangers at sea and is only completely happy when her loved ones are safely home on dry land.

She glances at the goodies, her afternoon's labour of love. They will keep. She doesn't feel like eating alone now. Disappointment has replaced her hunger. Please God, tomorrow we can all enjoy it. With a deep sigh of resignation, she rises and wearily climbs the stairs.

Friday

Morning is finally breaking. After a long night of deep, dark purgatory, the little group, drifting aimlessly in the vast Mediterranean, are clinging to what fragile tread of hope the dawn might bring. As the sun's warm face clears the horizon, slowly climbs the dome of blue sky, Paul assesses the state of his weary and dispirited crew. None had slept except Leo, who dozed off a few times, only to wake with a sudden jerk, survey the tragic scene, and then cry sobs of depression. Paul tries to console him, holding him close to keep him safe and warm.

Grandpa says his feet and legs are numb and his elbows and shoulders are aching. His suffering is reflected in the tortured look on his rapidly ageing face. Mario has perked up a bit with daylight. He is pre-occupied with the burden of keeping Ali focused and rational. It's becoming an impossible task. Ali keeps wailing: "I die...I die...water...I want water, water, water." Paul warns them all again that they must not drink seawater. He knows the pain of thirst will soon become intolerable. He also knows that to drink salt water to relieve it would be a death sentence. He scans the extremes of the vast, desolate ocean for signs of hope; he can see none. The water is calm and warming now. Apart from Ali's moans, the gentle lapping of the water against the floats is the only other sound. Still, this dawn brings hope for Paul. He tries to relay his optimism to his increasingly despairing crew.

"The search and rescue teams are out looking for us now. We are only about forty miles from Malta. The Armed Forces have several planes, helicopters, and boats. The Fishing boats from Bluegarr will be out too. Jason and Angelo will know where we are. They will be here soon; we should be home by mid-day."

*

Gabriella rises at six o'clock as usual, which gives her time for a few little jobs before walking the three hundred metres to the church for seven-thirty mass. Dom is still sleeping. She is not her usual sprightly self. Much of the night was spent lying awake wondering why Paul didn't arrive home.

As she enters the church, Father Borg is switching on the

electric fans in the ceiling with his remote control.

"Good Morning, Gabriella. How are you…and Paul…and the boys?" He spoke in a whisper.

"I'm worried, Father. The boat was due home yesterday and hasn't arrived. Paul took Grandpa and Leo with him.

He phoned to say they would be home on Thursday. Now it's Friday and I haven't heard from him since."

The priest sees the depth of anxiety in Gabriella's face.

"Oh please God, all will be well, Gabriella …don't worry too much yet …perhaps some little hold-up …maybe a simple explanation …We'll trust in the Lord."

"I can't help worrying, Father, it's not like Paul, something must have happened."

"We'll pray and please God you'll have news soon."

"Oh I really hope so …thank you Father."

She tries to pray fervently but her mind is firmly focussed on one thought. What could have happened?

Like a film slide-show, she can see a whole series of images flashing across her vision. Some of them are frightening which she quickly banishes and replaces with perfectly plausible scenarios.

After mass, she dwells for a few moments in front of the statue of Our Lady of Sorrows and silently places her family in the arms of Mary.

"Keep them in your loving care."

*

Mid-day in the simmering Mediterranean, the lonesome drifters are being pickled in the scorching sun. Its rays are beaming down so oppressively that their suffering, without a drop of drinking water, is becoming unbearable. The excruciating thirst, the distress of isolation with no sign of deliverance, the utter dejection of their spirits, fills them with deep despair and foreboding. As Paul gazes on the disconsolate faces of his parched and dehydrated comrades in suffering, he agonises on whether any of them can survive for long in these appalling conditions.

Why are we not being found? Why? Why? Why? His mind is in turmoil trying to comprehend the answer. Is anyone searching? It's twenty-four hours now since our radar and satellite instruments died. If they can't contact the 'St. Agatha', they must come and search for her. They will know her position from her last VMS signal. What is delaying them? Why are they not here?

Paul's strength of mind and ability to instil hope in the troubled minds of his crew is diminishing. Their second day of torment is ebbing away too. A few hours of daylight left and the dreaded prospect of another night of torture looms. Silently he prays to Jesus for deliverance.

"Lord, you saved your apostles on the Sea of Galilee, please come and save us now from this awful hell."

Ali is rapidly losing his strength and more worryingly, his sanity. He has lost his battle against the dreadful thirst and despite Mario's efforts, ravenously gulped the killer seawater into his dehydrated body. Now completely succumbed to despair, his will to endure this misery and suffering is gone. Ranting incoherently, he thrashes around, moaning from the agony of his thirst. Paul and Mario try to remonstrate with him but they are fighting a losing battle. He is delirious. How long can this torment continue?

Leo is now suffering the pangs of hunger and thirst. He is becoming really depressed, crying bitter tears and keeps calling for his Mummy. Paul's heart is breaking for his little suffering son. A glass of water or a biscuit would relieve his pain. He whispers another prayer.

"Oh Mother of Sorrows, please come to our aid."

*

It's a day of apprehension and worry for Gabriella. She has been trying to get through to her husband on the satellite phone but keeps getting the same 'engaged' tone as last night. If all is well with the 'St. Agatha' Paul and the crew will be in Bluegarr around six o'clock.

She is just managing to keep her anxieties under control. She

70

can't wait any longer. She rings her brother, George. He tells her not to be worrying. He will call over and drive her down to the harbour. It's almost six; the trawler should be unloading now. With typical loyalty George drops everything to help Gabriella.

Bluegarr Bay is quiet and peaceful. Few trawlers were deep sea fishing this week. Most were preparing for the lampuki season starting on Monday. Those that were out are in now and tied-up for the weekend. The 'St. Agatha' is the exception.

To the consternation of Gabriella and her brother, there is no sign of Paul. A sudden sensation of panic shoots through her. This confirms her worst fears. Something has happened to them. Her anguished eyes pierce the narrow gap of the harbour. There is nothing she can see to allay her intense trepidation. George holds her in a tender embrace. He agrees that she should contact the authorities.

*

The Armed Forces of Malta Operations Centre at Luqa Barracks is only ten minutes drive from Bluegarr Bay. George drives his trembling sister and her perplexed six-year-old son into the car park. He waits with Dom in the car as Gabreilla enters the building. She is received sympathetically. Her request for help is urgently acceded to. Details are logged by the Officer in-Charge. Within minutes, a search and rescue operation is set up. Gabriella feels a slight easing of her nervous tension. On the assurance of the AFM that she will be kept fully informed, she returns home with Dom and George to await developments and hopefully, some good news.

The Acting Commanding Officer of the Armed Forces of Malta Maritime Squadron, Major Tonio Bonnici takes charge of the search for the 'St. Agatha' Having failed to make contact with the vessel by all available means, he records her as officially missing at 6.30 p.m. In accordance with standard international procedures, he initiates a communications search. First, he must establish the exact last known position of the vessel.

The Armed Forces receive 'Vessel Monitoring System' signals but do not record them. They can only see where a boat is at a particular moment, but have no access to back-records. He contacts the Fisheries Department; the only department authorised to hold records of past positions of fishing boats. Requesting the last recorded position of the 'St Agatha', he is surprised and concerned with the information he receives.

"The last recorded signal received was 3 p.m. Thursday, placing her 33 miles from Malta, 53 miles off Filfl."

"Why was the absence of her normal two-hourly signal not noted and acted upon? Twenty-seven hours has now elapsed without a signal. Why no call to her satellite phone or VHF?"

The reply he receives disturbs him.

"The person who monitors these signals is on leave."

Driven by a new sense of urgency, the Officer contacts all Italian coast radio stations requesting them to try making contact with the 'St. Agatha'. He sends an alert message to all shipping, giving a detailed description of the vessel. He requests Libyan and Tunisian authorities to conduct enquiries to determine whether a Maltese fishing-vessel has entered one of their ports. He sends reports and descriptions of the overdue vessel to be broadcast repeatedly on Palermo Radio, Lampedusa Radio, and Malta Radio. A PAN-PAN message, which is a voice procedure giving a description of the missing boat is sent out to merchant vessel frequencies. One of the AFM patrol boats, P-51, returning from an incident involving irregular migrants close to Lampedusa is informed of the missing vessel and instructed to look out for it. An AFM aircraft on coastal patrol is told to look out for the overdue trawler.

*

Gabriella rings Paul's brother, Jason. He has been in port all day preparing his Lampuki floats for next week. He is astonished to hear that the 'St. Agatha' hasn't returned. He had spoken to Paul two days ago on VHF. Everything was fine then. They were getting shoals of fish and expected to be in early. He tells Gabriella not to worry too much.

"There could be many reasons why their communications have gone dead. Engine trouble would cause their delayed return. The AFM will have their exact position from the VMS. They will find them."

Although Jason is trying to convey to Gabriella an upbeat and positive air, he himself is stunned and worried at the news. The 'St. Agatha' is the newest boat in Bluegarr. She is fitted with the most modern equipment available. Something drastic must have happened to her. He phones his fishing partner, Angelo, who is also shocked and mystified.

He rings the Armed Forces. They say they have got a negative response to their communications search but it's too early to draw conclusions. A full-scale search using planes, helicopters and patrol boats is planned to begin at dawn. Jason is relieved to hear this. He contacts all the skippers of the Bluegarr fishing fleet. The immediate reaction is concern and fear for Paul and his crew. Jason tells them that if there is no news by morning he will be sailing at first light to search. They all pledge their full support. All boats will be ready. "We will sail, and not return 'til we find them."

*

In the heart of the cruel sea the little tortured, dispirited team are struggling heroically for survival. The red-faced sun is gently easing itself into the bed of the horizon. Darkness arrives to cast its gloomy spell. Another heartbreaking day has gone, leaving nothing to soothe the terrible anguish.

Ali's condition is now catastrophic. His physical and mental torment has reached a point of no return. His body is racked by dehydration. His mind is utterly dispirited and broken. His glassy, sunken eyes have the haunting look of death. He slips into unconsciousness. Mario is trying to keep him attached to the raft. It's now almost impossible as his lifeless body keeps sinking. He starts to wince and groan violently. His desiccated throat is now rasping its death rattle. Paul starts the rosary to Our Lady of Sorrows. The responses are a heartfelt pleading. Before the first mystery, 'The Agony in the Garden' is completed, Ali is delivered from the 'Agony in the Ocean'. He dies peacefully, and sinks gently into the silent tomb of a heartless, lonely sea.

Saturday

It's 5 a.m. Gabriella and her brother sip their umpteenth coffee. George is staying to support and comfort his sister through this terrible crisis. During the long and stressful night she has had two calls from the AFM. Sadly, they weren't able to give her any good news. "All elements of the 'communications search' report negative results." The commencement of a full-scale search and rescue operation at dawn is confirmed. Planes, helicopters and patrol boats will conduct a wide-ranging search. She will be kept informed of all relevant information. With George's calm, optimistic reasoning, Gabriella is clinging to hope that good news will emerge soon. She is convinced something serious has happened to the boat. Her dread is that her husband, son, father-in-law and the other two crewmen are in some danger. The boat can be replaced, her loved ones can't. She goes upstairs. As her little six-year-old son sleeps, her poignant gaze rest on his serene countenance. Anguish is melting her heart as she ponders the unthinkable.

Jason hasn't been to bed. His night was spent chain-smoking and agonising over the fate of his brother, father and nephew. He doesn't know the other crewmen well, but their safe return is equally important. There has never been a sea tragedy involving Maltese fishermen in his lifetime. The last one occurred in 1924, long before any of the present boatmen were born. There have been many near-tragedies and false alarms over the years. Trawlers have been overdue and reported missing many times. In almost all cases they were caught in unexpected storms. They always managed to return.

It's almost daylight. Jason rings Kenneth Galea, Secretary of the Fishermen's Co-Operative. He needs his help to organise the sea search. Kenneth will speak to the AFM. Their search would be more effective if done in collaboration with the AFM search. Jason agrees, says he has twenty boats ready to sail.

*

Dawn casts a hazy light over the dismal, unruffled Mediterranean. It doesn't bring any glimmer of light to the suffering souls clinging to life on their flimsy raft. Their torments have reached an unbearable level. Ali's death has sent their spirits plunging with him to the depths of the ocean. They now know the terrible fate that awaits them if they are not rescued soon. Dehydration and starvation will take them all. Grief and mourning intensifies their physical and mental anguish.

Mario is devastated by Ali's death. The agony and indignity of his demise is haunting his every thought. They were more than shipmates, they were friends. During long intimate chats on their work breaks, Ali had confided in Mario his boyhood hardships in Somalia, his lucky escape to Malta, his hopes for the future. He was really happy with his new life. Now he is no more. This intolerable grief, the overpowering pain of thirst, the utter futility of the struggle for survival, has wrenched all hope from Mario. He is now near to total despair, resigned to his sad, inevitable destiny.

Paul's own suffering is overshadowed by his loving care and nurturing of Leo. Cradling and hugging him, chatting about Mummy and Dom, keeping him as cheerful and comfortable as possible, all help to ease the pain of hunger and thirst racking his fragile body. It is also distracting Paul from his own distress.

His father is suffering in silence. His feet are numb, his legs are locked in terrible cramp, his mouth and throat scaled and raw from the burning thirst. He is not complaining. He has lived sixty-seven good years. He has no fear of death, but he is determined to cling to life as long as hope and breath remain in him. His continuous silent prayers are sustaining him.

As the sun rises, Paul's weary eyes scan the curved horizon for a speck of hope that might develop into a vessel of deliverance. Sadly, nothing but an endless expanse of gloom and heartbreak surrounds him. He tries to contemplate the reason why they are not being found.

'We were due home on Thursday. It's Saturday now, surely a search for us is underway. They will be searching for the boat. The boat is gone. They will assume that where the boat is, we will be too. They will not be searching for a tiny raft; a mere dot in the ocean. If we even had a flare or anything to attract attention, it might save us. The only item we have is the white towel that we used for a mask on the boat. It is not much but we could wave it if a plane or helicopter was overhead.'

Paul's thoughts turn to his wife and little son at home. What must Gabriella be suffering at this moment? Her mental anguish must be as bad as ours. Dom will be protected from the true extent of the crisis. George will be with his sister in her ordeal. He will look after her and ease her pain. He has always been a true friend to her.

Jason too, will be concerned and apprehensive. He is probably out searching now. Having been down here fishing many times, he will know where to come. The 'Blue Horizon' would be a welcome sight now.

"Oh Sacred Heart of Jesus, guide and direct him to us."

*

Bluegarr Bay awakens to the heightened debate of bewildered, agitated fishermen. They have assembled on the pier waiting for instructions to sail. Jason and Angelo have the 'Blue Horizon' ready to lead. All are waiting for the Fisheries Co-Op Secretary, Kenneth Galea, to arrive with the co-ordinated plan.

As his jeep screeches to a halt, a frustrated Kenneth slams the door, runs down the pier wall, addresses the fishermen.

"I have just been to the AFM Headquarters. They have assumed full control of the search and rescue operation. A full-scale search is already underway. The AFM Islander planes are taking part, along with an Italian Air Force AB212 helicopter from the Italian Military Mission in Malta. Also involved is a Tunisian search-helicopter, a Sigonella-based Italian Navy Atlantique and a US Navy 6th Fleet P3-Orion aircraft.

They have advised that the search operation be conducted exclusively by the Armed Forces. They say that uncoordinated searches would not be beneficial, might even be hazardous. They will maintain close co-operation with me, as the representative of the fishermen, during all stages of the operation."

The fishermen listen attentively to the words of their respected spokesman. They appreciate his efforts on their behalf. Without one dissenting voice, all vehemently disagree with the AFM. Jason is livid.

"Three members of my family are out there. We know the area. We know the currents. We must be allowed to search for them." Kenneth tries to explain the AFM's decision.

"They believe there is more probability of finding the boat by air than by sea. This involve considerations such as the speed at which air craft and sea craft travel and the distances that could be covered."

Jason and his angry colleagues are not convinced. They recall previous emergencies when the AFM air searches failed to locate stricken fishermen. It was the fishing boatmen with their skill and experience that always came to the rescue. After heated debate the fishermen agree a compromise. They will stay in port today and await developments. If the 'St. Agatha' is not found by to-morrow morning, they will ignore the advice of the AFM and steam to the search area. "Agreed!"

*

It's 11 a.m. on a sultry July morning. Staff Sergeant Darrin Muscat climbs into the cockpit of his 'Islander' aircraft and prepares for take off. Beside him his co-pilot, Warrant Officer Ivan Agius; behind is the flight technician, Gunner Mark Saliba.

Two 'Islanders' are based at the AFM Air Wing. One has just

landed, having been airborne for a fruitless five hours, searching the Mediterranean for the 'St. Agatha'. Darrin hopes for better luck. Two planes from the Italian and US Navy and two helicopters are taking part in the search, backed up by the AFM patrol boats P51 and P52.

Darrin is allocated an area of 2000 square nautical miles. Cleared by the 'tower', he takes off. At 500 feet he raises the flaps. Slowly, she gains speed as the nose is lowered at 1000 feet. She turns for the coast. The 'tower' hands him over to the radar controller, who clears him to the search area. He continues to climb to 3000 feet.

The weather over the sea is not good. A thick haze makes the horizon indistinguishable. The sea is almost invisible below them. Thirty miles from Malta he notices the AFM's P52 sailing at speed in the same direction.

Approaching the search area, the co-pilot tunes the radar, Darrin starts his descent into the thick haze below.   Levelling the plane at 1000 feet, Ivan gets busy with the radar, alert for any tiny contact that may appear. Mark, the tech in the back, is scanning with the FLIR, through the haze, seeing what the men in front can't.

 As the 'Islander' repeatedly criss-cross the hot, murky ocean, Darrin and his crew are suffering the effects of the sultry conditions. The sky is almost featureless. The haze and heat are oppressive, their eyes are weary from the constant vigil of looking outside.

After three hours of fruitless searching, Darrin takes stock. Levelling the wings, he calculates how much fuel he has left. He should be able to stay in the area for another hour and a half. The co-pilot concurs. Back in search mode, Darrin is busy switching his attention between looking outside and monitoring the gauges. Ivan is managing to look outside and also scan the radar screen. Mark has his eyes firmly fixed on the FLIR monitor. They are all looking for that slightest telltale, the faintest indication that something is out there in the murk. A sudden yell from Darrin; he has spotted something. He points to his left. Just outside his search area there is a dot, slightly darker than the surrounding sea, about four miles away. His eyes fix on the contact as he turns towards it. The radar shows no contact but Darrin flies on, determined to make sure. He checks with Mark to see if the FLIR shows anything. Nothing. Just then, Darrin loses visual contact with the object.

He marks the position on the GPS. It will give him a reference as he continues to fly in its direction. With all eyes firmly focused on the water, they circle the area several times but to no avail. It has disappeared.

Just as they are about to give up and turn back to their search pattern, Darrin spots the contact again. It is right below them.

Amazingly, they almost missed it. Instantly, the tech in the back reports that he has visual contact on a boat directly below them. The co-pilot hits the GPS mark button and Darrin sends the Islander into a tight left turn to avoid losing visual contact again. At 200 feet, he continues to orbit the boat. The occupants wave an assortment of items to attract attention. He angles in towards them at less than 100 feet at as slow a speed as possible, giving the tech in the back the best view possible for photographs. The aircraft wallows at the high engine settings and slow speed. On board the crippled 15 foot boat are 30 people; Somalia immigrants, marooned and helpless on their way to Malta.

Ivan is on the radio informing the Operations Centre as Darrin climbs the aircraft into orbit over the boat. He re-calculates how much longer they can stay in the area; not very long. A call comes from the control room. "Return to base. The patrol boat P52 is only 30 minutes away, with the migrant boat contacts on its radar."

Darrin swings the Islander back towards Malta, 40 miles away, re-tunes the navigational instruments. He adds some more power, puts the aircraft into a gentle climb, heading at high cruise power for home. Staff Sergeant Darrin Muscat and his 'Islander' crew are disappointed at their failure to find the 'St. Agatha'. They are happy that they have probably saved the lives of 30 human beings.

*

In the heart of the lonely, anonymous ocean, three men and a boy languish beneath a sultry, afternoon sky. With no way to screen themselves from the sun's scorching rays, their suffering is reaching a new, agonising level. The extreme oppression of the heat, the absence of the slightest sign of deliverance, the deterioration of their physical and mental condition, fills them with foreboding of their inevitable, cruel destiny.

Paul is dismayed by the total collapse of Mario's resolve to struggle on. Despite his pleadings, his once 'rock of strength' now feeds his burning thirst with ravenous mouthfuls of seawater. Paul knows that this is like pouring petrol on a smouldering fire. He tries to comfort and console him but Mario isn't listening. He is totally dispirited and broken down.

Grandpa is grimly holding on to his dignity and focus. Despite his age and the extremity of his sufferings he is remarkably calm and forbearing. Paul is motivated and inspired by his resilience to endure such misery and distress. Leo's comfort and wellbeing is foremost in Grandpa's mind. He tries to speak a few words of encouragement to his little fragile grandson, but speech is increasingly difficult from his saliva-starved mouth.

Paul is pre-occupied too with Leo's health and welfare. The little boy's body is becoming emaciated, his strength rapidly evaporating. He is sleeping a lot. He dreams of eating food, then wakes to further agony. When awake, he cries for food and water. His father keeps talking to him, distracting him from the pain of his hunger and thirst. Paul hasn't slept for three days. He is determined to stay awake, giving protection and tender loving care to his precious little son.

Three days of drifting helplessly in this Limbo of misery has failed to crush Paul's faith that God will deliver them. He feels a solemn duty to his crew, especially to his young son, to soldier on. He will never distrust the providence of the Lord or give himself up to despair. He will continue to believe that somehow, their tribulations will end and they will be snatched from this sea of peril. Throughout his life, at times of doubt, difficulty or danger, his greatest advocate has never let him down. His simple prayer would always be:

"Sacred Heart of Jesus, I place all my trust in Thee."

*

Gabriella is distraught with anguish and trepidation. George is doing his best to comfort and console her. Another day is drawing to a close without any news of her loved ones. The tension is unbearable. Neighbours are calling to enquire and offer support. The Armed Forces have been giving her agonising, negative updates of the search. Dom keeps asking when is Dad, Leo and Grandpa coming home? She is trying to contend with all this turmoil and the chaos of her own emotions.

The Church of Our Lady of Sorrows is aptly named for the vigil mass this Saturday evening. The overflowing congregation of fishermen and their families have one petition: the safe return of the 'St. Agatha' and her crew. A dark cloud of worry and apprehension is hovering above Bluegarr Bay. No boats have left the harbour today. Bewilderment and frustration is dominating the thoughts and expressions of the fishing community. This evening, they are filling the church to pray. To-morrow, they will be searching the vast Mediterranean for their friends. Nothing will stop them from sailing at first light. They will not return until their colleagues are found.

A tense atmosphere of foreboding is palpable throughout the church. Concern and apprehension is etched on the faces of the faithful. At times of grief and sorrow these devout souls always turn to prayer. This evening they are united in their heartfelt plea.

Father Borg offers comfort and empathy to Gabriella. He assures her of the fervent prayers of himself and the whole community. He announces to the congregation that the vigil mass is being offered especially for the safe return of Paul and his crew. Gabriella is fortified by this generous outpouring of solidarity, prayers and support. Before leaving the church she visits the little shrine of 'Our Lady of Sorrows'.

Kneeling in silence, the *'Finding of the Child Jesus in the Temple'* comes to her mind. She whispers her heartfelt plea:

"Mother Mary, please find my family for me"

*

The light of a third day is almost extinguished. Darkness casts its dismal cloak over the suffering souls of the sea. Mario's light of hope is now firmly quenched. His head, and face are swollen, his body blistered from the violent sun, having given his jacket to protect Leo. His thirst has reached an agonising degree, his shrivelled mouth has ceased to produce saliva, his voice can speak no more.

Paul is devastated to watch helplessly as Mario suffers this terrible ordeal of pain and affliction. He constantly speaks words of comfort and encouragement to him, but nothing can now soothe his inner torments of gloom and despondency. His mind is dark and desolate, drained of the last drop of hope. He has no strength or will left to continue the struggle for life. He is now resigned to the relief of his inevitable destiny.

In a spontaneous, wild twist of his parched body, a loud cry of anguish, and a sudden splash, he is gone from the raft, into the lonely grave of the silent ocean.

This new surge of grief and mourning, the intense darkness of the night, the dread and apprehension of their fate, all combine to fill Paul with extreme confusion and sadness. His anguish is almost unbearable. The awful climax to Mario's young life is a sword through his heart. He feels a guilt and responsibility for the loss of a bright and ambitious young life. His thoughts are now filled with heartfelt compassion for Mario's frail mother. His life was so unselfishly devoted to her. Now she has lost her only consolation. Paul finds it hard to comprehend God's rationale in acquiescing to all this grief and heartbreak.

"Oh God, what have we done to deserve this awful punishment?"

Sunday

Dawn is breaking over a sombre Bluegarr Bay. As the gloomy darkness lifts, a flotilla of twenty boats sail out on a mission of mercy. Sixty fishermen, focussed and determined, man the decks for this voyage of mystery and unknown. Bluegarr's dedicated rescue team are disturbed by their enforced, delayed entry into the search operation. They fear that valuable time has been lost, while their colleagues, battling with adversity, have been left isolated and abandoned.

'The Blue Horizon' is leading the armada of hope. Jason, bewildered, tormented and angry, is at the helm. When they reach the search area he will hand over to Angelo, allowing him to scan every inch of water. He doesn't know what grim discovery awaits him. He is prepared for exhilaration or devastation. He is determined to locate something. Hopefully, it will be the 'St Agatha' with her crew safe and well. But it could be wreckage, survivors or even bodies. Hope, tinged with apprehension, fills his mind as he ponders the unpredictable outcome of the hours and days ahead.

*

The mystery of the missing trawler is headline news in the daily papers of Malta and neighbouring countries. The 'Times of Malta' has a front page banner headline:

"AFM SEARCHING FOR OVERDUE FISHING VESSEL".

"The Armed Forces of Malta are searching for a Maltese-registered fishing vessel with five persons on board after it was reported overdue yesterday."

A picture shows: *"An 'Islander' aircraft, returning, from two fruitless searches of the Mediterranean."*

The 'Malta Independent' headline reads:

"US NAVY JOINS IN SEARCH FOR MISSING FISHERMEN"

"A US Navy P-3 Orion maritime patrol aircraft yesterday joined Maltese and Italian patrols searching for a Maltese fishing vessel, reported missing by concerned family members, following the crew's failure to return to port. The search at first concentrated on the area west of Malta and south of

Lampedusa, but has now been extended to cover a wider area. Search efforts were ongoing as of yesterday evening."

Maltese Radio and Television also give progress reports of the search in their hourly bulletins. The identity of the trawler and the names of its crew are being withheld, but by now are well known in every fishing port in Malta.

*

At the invitation of Major Tonio Bonnici, Acting Commanding Officer of the AFM Maritime Squadron, Gabriella goes to the headquarters in Haywharf for a briefing on the progress of the search. George waits in the car as his distraught sister enters the building. Major Bonnici gives a full report and appraisal of the search. He expresses his regret that despite the deployment of the full resources of the AFM, as yet, no positive outcome has resulted. He assures Gabriella that the search will continue relentlessly and will be intensified if necessary. She thanks him, requests that her gratitude be conveyed to the officers and troops for their untiring, dedicated efforts. Major Bonnici sees her out with the assurance that "no effort will be spared in the search to find the crew. She will be kept fully informed of all relevant developments."

On their way home, George makes a slight diversion. Gabriella wants to visit Mario's mother, Grace, who lives at the opposite end of Bluegarr. Since her fisherman husband died seven years ago, only Grace and Mario occupy the neat little dwelling at the bottom of the narrow street. Grace has been in poor health since she suffered a stroke last year. At first she was totally incapacitated, but has made a partial recovery. She is mobile now with the aid of a walking frame, an achievement that greatly cheers her. She is improving slowly, but one side of her body is still weak; she finds it difficult to speak clearly. All of Mario's time when ashore, is devoted to caring for his mother. Her sister, Valerie, who lives nearby, is also a guardian angel to Grace, caring for her when Mario is away fishing.

Since news broke of the disappearance of the 'St Agatha', Grace has been praying non-stop. The radio news keeps her informed of the search. Father Borg and all the neighbours have been in to offer prayers, support and encouragement. She refuses to believe that the boat and her crew will not be found. In her sixty years of memory, many boats and fishermen have gone missing.

"Faith and prayer have always brought them back."

Gabriella has a cup of tea with Grace. She tells of her trip to the AFM and the progress of the search. They talk about the wonderful gesture of the fishermen, sailing en masse on their mission of true solidarity. Grace talks about Mario, her life's joy.

"A son in a million. What would I do without him?"

With a tender, loving embrace, Gabriella leaves, strengthened and encouraged by the remarkable spirit of Grace. An inspiring example of dignity, faith and bravery, in the midst of such fear and trepidation.

*

Four days of torment has not diminished Paul's resolve to cling to hope in the face of a cruel complication of disasters. As the oppressive sun beams down on the decimated group, doomed to perish in their bowl of misery, he knows that only a miracle will save them now. He is prepared to suffer on as long as his human endurance will last, determined to protect his young son, now weak, but cradled comfortably in his arms.

The sea is calm and smooth. Not a breath of wind or a rippling wave to disturb the eerie silence of this aquarium of death. Paul's sad, weary eyes scan the endless table of grey glass. Around the vast curve of horizon there is nothing but a monotonous sheet of empty sea. The awful pain of isolation, abandonment, and impending doom is weighing him down with depression and an increasing sense of hopelessness. He will not surrender to despair. Perhaps today, God will come to their aid, rescue them from this horror.

Paul is now resigned to the imminent loss of his father. It's a heartbreaking prospect, but only a rescue in the next few hours will save him. Though bravely uncomplaining, Grandpa is fading rapidly. His aged body, starved and dehydrated, is now completely worn out, unable to absorb further hardship and deprivation. His mind is still lucid, but his ability to speak is long gone. Comforting words from Paul are responded to with eye and facial gestures of gratitude and resignation.

Paul is conscious that his father's brave fight for life is linked to his love and concern for Leo. Since his wife and soul mate, Maria, died, he seemed to transfer all his affection to his grandson. Leo too, has a special love for Grandpa. Now, tragically, fate has twinned them in these waters of heartbreak. Their earthly bond of love is about to be broken. With a heavy heart, Paul is fearful that soon, it may be restored in Heaven.

*

It's mid-day; twenty boats are sixty miles south west of Malta. They are all in VHF contact; ready to comb the Mediterranean in search of their friends and colleagues. They will sail abreast half a mile apart. Each strip searched will be thirty miles long by ten miles wide. The water is calm; the sun is sweltering from a cloudless, blue sky. Jason is leading in 'The Blue Horizon.' He is aware that the AFM planes have already searched this area. They state that they have covered 3900 square nautical miles. He accepts that if the 'St. Agatha' was here the AFM would have found her.

"But they were searching for a boat; we are searching for the crew. Surface searches are better than air searches."

Jason suspects something catastrophic must have happened to the trawler causing her to sink. In that event the crew would have taken to the life raft. The 'St. Agatha' has an inflatable, fully equipped life raft that can hold six people. It has flares, food, water and medical requirements, that would sustain the crew for many days. Although it would be only a tiny speck in the ocean, its bright orange colour would help locate it.

All the fishermen in the search team agree with Jason's theory. Hawk-eyed, they sail ahead, alert for the tiniest speck of anything that will lead them to their friends. They know the magnitude of the task ahead of them. The Mediterranean is a vast area of anonymous water. If Paul and his crew were in a life raft, they may have drifted as much as sixty miles from their last known position. Undaunted, the fishermen press on, prepared for a long, frustrating search. If it takes a week they won't mind if their efforts bring their brothers home safe and well.

*

Through four days and nights of anguish, Paul has sustained himself with faith, and a resolve to cling to life as long as breath remained in him. He will not abandon hope that God will spare him and his son even at the heartbreaking cost of losing his father and the rest of his crew. His mind cannot comprehend the incredible fact that for four long, dismal days and nights, no one has managed to find them. He knows how minuscule they are in the vastness of the ocean. He knows they have nothing to attract attention. No flares, no light, no bright colours, nothing. But even if they had all these things, it wouldn't have mattered. No planes, no helicopters, no boats, no one has come to search for them. It's a sad, depressing feeling of isolation and abandonment that grips Paul as he faces another night of dark torture.

Grandpa is slowly passing away. For the past two days, hope was all that stood between him and death. His aged body, decimated by hunger and thirst, is in its last moments of life. Starvation and dehydration have combined to wreak havoc on his internal organs; he is now slipping away peacefully.

As darkness shrouds the lonely, grey seascape, Grandpa closes his tired eyes for the last time and without a murmur, gives up his spirit, in a gentle, dignified release. A sword of new torture again pierces Paul's heart. His guilt and heartbreak at seeing his father endure this terrible suffering is eased slightly by his peaceful, painless end. He was worn out; the breath just left his body. Now he must turn all his attention to his son, grieving for his beloved Grandpa.

Paul ties the polystyrene strips more firmly to his father's upper arms, releasing him from the raft. This allows his body to drift away slowly in a 'dead man's float'. It is heartbreaking, but it will enhance the possibility of his body being found.

The little boy is physically very weak but surprisingly strong and calm mentally in accepting Grandpa's death. Paul tries to raise his spirits, giving him hope that soon they will be rescued.

"God has taken Grandpa to a new life, a happier life."

"I know," whispered Leo. "He will take us too."

"Why do you say that, Son?"

"It's like the Sea of Galilee. God fills our boat with fish and then takes us to a new life."

Paul is astounded. Since Grandpa's body drifted away, he notices a new angelic serenity in his little son's face. The terror is gone from his eyes, his reflexes are more relaxed, and he seems resigned to God's little plan for him.

*

It's the end of a frustrating day for Jason and his team. Twenty boats, sixty fishermen, one hundred and twenty sharp eyes, have found no trace of the 'St. Agatha' or her crew. They have seen planes, helicopters, AFM patrol boats, but nothing of Paul and his crew. As darkness halts the search, Jason ponders two possibilities. To-day's search was in the general area of the last recorded VMS position of the 'St. Agatha' She may have travelled for two hours from that position before something happened to her. In that case we were searching the wrong area. If her mishap occurred in the area of her last recorded position, causing her to sink and her crew to board the life raft, they may have drifted for fifty or sixty miles.

Either of those scenarios would explain why we failed to locate them today, would provide renewed hope that we can find them to-morrow. It's fifteen hours since the boats left Bluegarr this morning. They will now rest and resume at dawn. The fishermen are tired and weary. They need food and a few hours of sleep.

*

Gabriella is drained and worn out from the feverish restlessness of her body and the utter turmoil of her mind. Her day has been spent feigning calm and optimism when little Dom is around, crying and praying when alone. George is keeping her sane and focussed. But for his loyal, solid support, she could not have survived. She appreciates his brotherly love.

The AFM have called to say they have no good news to relate. All their resources are deployed, but as yet, no sightings have been made. The search will resume at first light in the morning.

Jason is on his satellite phone giving Gabriella an update on the fishermen's day. After seven hours searching the area of the last recorded position of the 'St. Agatha', they failed to find any trace of the boat or the crew. To-morrow at dawn, they will begin searching an adjoining area. "The next time I call, I hope to have good news."

Little Dom now knows that something serious has happened to Dad's boat. The radio and television reports are now naming the vessel and her crew. Gabriella and George keep telling him that the boat has been delayed, will be home soon. As time passes and his Mummy's state of anxiety worsens, he is becoming unsure and unconvinced. It's a long time since he has talked to Dad, Leo and Grandpa. He misses them a lot, can't wait to see them.

Monday

The cheerful face of the rising sun casts its brightness over the grey, dismal Mediterranean. Its warm glow help to ease the memory of a bitterly cold, cruel night of misery for Paul and his little son. The warmth is welcome, but the pain of loneliness and isolation of an empty, desolate seascape, negate what little comfort it brings.

It's a bright new day, but for Paul and Leo, drifting aimlessly, clinging to life, it's another step closer to death or deliverance. As he cradles his little fragile son, he knows their sufferings are drawing to a close. A terrible death or a miracle rescue awaits them. Ali, Mario and Grandpa, three strong men, have failed to survive this cruel suffering. Leo has survived because of the little comfort and care he has been given. Paul knows that he has kept Leo alive. But he also knows that Leo has kept him alive. His courage, his strength, his resolve, his refusal to abandon hope, has all come from his brave little son.

Paul laments the irony of his tragic situation. An ocean of water surrounds them. If only he could find one glass of drinking water, he would save his son. A sea full of every shape and size of fish surrounds them. If only he could catch one little fish it would be a lifesaver.

Leo is so weak he can't stay awake for more than a few minutes. His body is completely dehydrated, his mouth and tongue are parched, starved of saliva, his eyes are tearless and empty. Paul's own sufferings are wearing him down. His hunger pangs are unbearable. His body is in agony from the ravages of extreme dehydration. His mouth, tongue and throat are hard and crusted. He hasn't slept for four days and nights, fearful of neglecting Leo. The calf muscles of his legs and his lower body are raw and painful, from the prolonged immersion in salt water. His head is scorched and blistered, his face baked and peeling, his arms are weak and aching, just strong enough to hold Leo in a safe, comfortable position.

How long more will he be able to endure this torment and deprivation? He has asked himself that question many times. The answer is getting progressively shorter, more depressing.

Paul feels he should now ask a different question. How long more can Leo survive? If he loses his son, the question of his own survival will be answered. His will to live will be gone. His courage and spirit will be extinguished. He will not want to be the lucky survivor of a loyal crew that shared such suffering and death.

His eyes are almost closing, but he continues to circle the endless ocean in a pained, weary sweep. The empty feeling of abandonment is killing him. He studies his little sleeping son, contentedly waiting for God's beckoning hand. His mind fills with the image of Grandpa, waiting in Heaven with open arms ready to hug and embrace his little pride and joy. Paul would be happy to be present for that 'Heavenly' welcome. But it is not for him to decide. They have all been afflicted with this terrible burden of suffering and purgatory. God will decide if they are all to fulfil the same destiny.

"Jesus, Mary and Joseph, assist us now and in our last agony."

*

Gabriella, Dom and George enter the Church of Our Lady of Sorrows, for a special Mass offered for the safe return of the 'St. Agatha' and her crew. Father Borg greets them with compassion and sympathy. The church is full with a community of worried parishioners, petrified and fervently praying for some good news.

Mario's invalid mother, Grace, wheeled up the church by her sister, Valerie, sits in her wheelchair before the high alter. It's her first Mass since suffering her stroke almost a year ago, but despite medical disapproval, insists on being present. Gabriella embraces her, whispering a few consoling words.

Before mass begins, Father Borg speaks words of encouragement and solidarity. He recalls the gospel story when Jesus and his disciples were on the Sea of Galilee.

"And there arose a great storm of wind, and the waves beat into the boat. And Jesus was in the hinder part of the boat, asleep on a pillow: and they awake him, Master, carest thou not that we perish?

And he arose, and rebuked the wind, and said unto the sea, Peace, be still. And the wind ceased, and there was a great calm.

And he said unto them, Why are you so fearful? How is it that you have so little faith?"

"My dear brethren, we are fearful, we are worried and we are concerned. But our presence here today, and the heroic efforts of our men at sea, shows that we have faith. Faith in Jesus Christ, that like the disciples on the Sea of Galilee, our brothers will be found, and return safe to their families and community."

After Mass, the congregation huddle in little groups outside the church. All are anxious to offer support and empathy to

Gabriella and Grace. Words of hope, encouragement and optimism are expressed sincerely. There is no mention of shipwreck, drowning or death, but though not expressed, these dreaded terms are lurking below the surface of their minds.

Grace eases her frail body from the wheelchair to a standing position beside her sister's car. She takes a long, sad look at the empty dock, her first for almost a year. Her heart fills with gratitude to all the fishermen that are tirelessly searching the sea.

"Heart of Jesus, Fount of Love and Mercy, bring them home safe."

Slowly the little groups disperse. Gabriella has had a word with all. She walks towards the car. George is waiting. Dom isn't there. In panic, she exclaims: "Where's Dom?"

George says he thought he was with her outside the church. They run in opposite directions, Gabriella back towards the church, George down towards the pier.

Dom is found standing on the furthest point of the pier wall. His little anxious eyes are searching the sea. George takes him gently by the hand back to his Mummy.

"Why did you leave us like that, Dom? You know you shouldn't. We were worried about you."

"I was just looking for Dad and Leo and Grandpa."

She wipes the tears from his little cheeks, hugs him, before drying the stream flowing from her own eyes.

*

The headline in the 'Times of Malta' reads:

"NO SIGN OF MISSING BOAT"

"The Armed Forces of Malta are working closely with the Libyan and Tunisian authorities who have searched their waters in an attempt to find the Maltese fishing boat reported missing almost a week ago.

The intensive search for the 12-metre-long 'St.Agatha' and her five crewmembers, including an 11-year-old boy, has been going on since the vessel was reported overdue on Friday. So far there has been no sign of the vessel. The AFM and the Italian Military Mission in Malta have worked with the Italian Navy and the US Navy to look for the fishing boat over the past five days.

Twenty fishing vessels have also set out to search for the 'St. Agatha' and are in regular contact with the AFM."

The 'Malta Independent' headline says:

"SEARCH FOR FISHING BOAT CONTINUES"

"Searches continued yesterday for the overdue fishing vessel 'St. Agatha' and its five-man crew. The AFM Air Wing's Islander aircraft and the locally-based Italian Air Force AB 212 Search-and-Rescue helicopter of the Italian military mission conducted morning searches, while Sigonella-based Italian Navy Atlantique aircraft and a US Navy P3-Orion

aircraft conducted afternoon searches, but all with no results"

*

The searing mid-day sun bakes the fishermen, watching from twenty oven-hot decks. They have been scouring the massive seascape since early dawn, without sight or sign of Paul and his crew. Jason is in constant contact with his colleagues on VHF, but all have drawn a blank. For Jason, it's demoralising and heartrending. They have now searched the total area of the last recorded position. They have studied the currents of the past week and calculated the direction and distance of drift. They have searched that wide area without trace. He is baffled; it's a mystery. The 'St. Agatha' has completely vanished.

Jason receives a call on the satellite phone from Major Bonnici, Search Co-ordinator at AFM Marine Squadron.

"Debris has been sighted by one of our aircraft."

It's near the general area being searched by the fishermen. Jason responds immediately. Steaming to the location, his heart is racing with adrenaline and apprehension. Is this evidence of a disaster or a breakthrough that will lead them to the stricken crew?

Jason locates the debris, or flotsam, as the fishermen call it. Strewn over a wide area it appears as if it is from a sunken boat. Each item is examined and re-examined for absolute certainty.

Jason is positive the flotsam is not from the 'St. Agatha. He calls Major Bonnici to inform him. On his way back to join the team he reflects in the anti-climax of the false alarm. He is relieved that he didn't find evidence of a sunken 'St. Agatha'. He is mindful that some ill-fated boat may have sunk there; perhaps unfortunate, irregular migrants, on their way to a new life in Malta. He is still optimistic that Paul and his crew didn't suffer a similar fate and that a real breakthrough will soon emerge.

*

As evening approaches on his fifth day of agony, Paul is now convinced that it is his destiny to die. If another ghostly night descends without deliverance from this dungeon, Leo will be gone and he will soon follow.

He knows his internal organs are deteriorating rapidly. His strength is leaving him. He is struggling to stay awake and protect Leo. His mind is beginning to fill with pessimistic, melancholy thoughts. The awful feeling of abandonment is intensifying his mental distress.

Leo is now constantly in a slumber of weakness. He cannot speak but when awake he communicates with his little sickly eyes. Sometimes he even manages a loving wan smile for his heartbroken Dad. Paul knows the end is near for his little son. He is perplexed and mystified by God's decision to ordain him with this vocation of torture. His faith reminds him that "God's ways are not our ways." He studies the serene countenance of his little dying son. A consoling prayer of resignation crosses his troubled mind:

"Thy Will be Done on Earth as it is in Heaven."

Paul is jerked from his pensive sadness by the sound of an aircraft in the distance. He searches the blue dome, sees a helicopter approaching in his direction. A feeling of elation and gratitude to God fills his being. He wakes Leo and grabs the white towel he has been saving for this moment. As the helicopter approaches it descends in altitude and circles the raft. He cannot read the markings. Its identity doesn't matter. All that matters now is that their long suffering is at an end. The noise above their heads is deafening. Paul frantically waves the towel and shouts as loud as his hoarse voice can:

"Maltese! Maltese! Maltese! We are Maltese!"

To his consternation, bewilderment and heartbreak, the helicopter ascends in altitude, accelerates its engine and flies away. Paul is devastated. His tear-filled eyes turn from the disappearing dot in the distance, to rest on Leo's little sad face. He embraces his son in a hug of anguish, knowing that his last hope of survival has flown away into the distance of a heartless blue sky.

Paul is now convinced they are doomed to perish. To feel their frenzied elation of gratitude and joy shattered by this humiliation is the ultimate torture in their whole catalogue of sufferings. He doesn't want to add to his torment by trying to make sense of why they were rejected, forsaken and left to die. In the darkness of his mind, where hope has now taken a crushing blow, he can't help feeling that for five days he has been struggling in a mission impossible, fighting against their preordained, inevitable destiny.

***

Tuesday

A faint shade of brightness on the curved horizon marks the end of the longest and most distressing night for Paul. The intense darkness, the eerie silence, the monotonous sound of the ice-cold water lapping around him, all adds to the extreme misery of his tormented mind. Through the dark gloom he tries to ponder the logic behind this relentless, cruel, litany of disasters placed before him. He feels that even at this eleventh hour, he deserves a reprieve. He doesn't feel guilty of any serious misdeed that would warrant this sentence of terrible punishment. It's now bright enough to study the emaciated face of his little dying son. Leo is now semiconscious, his skin is ashen grey, his breathing strained and erratic; he is shifting restlessly. Paul is cradling him gently to his breast, but can now feel the life draining from him with every passing minute. His little mouth is so hard and dry, it looks sealed. Paul tries to transfer with his finger a little saliva from his own parched mouth. A feather, dipped in water would now prolong his little son's life. It's a heartbreaking thought that compounds the pain in every fibre of his being.

Leo's breathing is now course and irregular. His movement has ceased. His eyes are closed and peaceful. The pain of hunger and thirst seems to have left him. He appears serene, content and tranquil. The pauses between breaths are now longer. Paul shares every breath, knowing there are not many left. Without a murmur or a movement, the breathing ceases. Paul's breathing stops too. He waits; listens. Feverish shock bolts through him. A paralysing wave of anguish crashes through his mind. Hazy disbelieve soon evolves into cruel reality. Agonisingly embracing Leo, he listens again. Silence, except for the dismal lapping water, now playing an unbearable lament. Little Leo has gone to find Grandpa and renew their special love and affection in a new, happier life.

*

Gabriella hasn't slept a wink all night. Every possible calamity to afflict her loved ones has been felt and endured by her troubled mind during the long hours of darkness and depression. Though worn out, she is eager to face this new day clinging to a precarious tread of hope. "This can't continue. Please God, today something will emerge to lift this pall of trepidation and suffering."

During the long, tearful night, she has prayed incessantly. To Almighty God, to The Sacred Heart of Jesus, to The Holy Spirit, to Our Blessed Lady, Mother of Sorrows. This morning she is going to plead with the saint who, over the centuries, has been a true friend to Malta: Saint Paul. It was to Malta that Paul struggled ashore when shipwrecked on his way from Jerusalem to Rome, in 60 AD.

The Bible quotes Paul:

"I have faith in God that it will be as I have been told.

We shall have to run on some island.

After we escaped we then learned that the island was called Malta.

The natives showed us unusual kindness.

The people of the island who had diseases came and were cured. And when we sailed they put on board whatever we needed." (Acts of the Apostles)

During his three-month stay on the island, Paul preached the word of Jesus, healed the sick, and gave Malta the Christian faith, which has been cherished ever since. St Paul has long been the patron saint of Malta; the people revere and venerate him in a special way.

George drives Gabriella to St. Paul's Bay, to the little chapel built on the spot where Paul came ashore. She enters the tiny 'Church of the Shipwreck of St. Paul.' Kneeling before the large canvas, by Cassarino, depicting the shipwreck and Paul's stepping ashore, Gabriella studies the scene. In silent contemplation she blends the trauma of Paul's shipwreck almost 2000 years ago with the tragic plight of her loved ones in the very same waters at this sad moment.

"Please St. Paul, you, who battled and survived these waters, help Paul, Leo, Grandpa, Mario and Ali to return safely ashore as you did on this sacred spot."

She lights five little red candles. They flicker gently before the altar; her five missing souls glowing with life. The little flames will extinguish one by one and be no more. She prays that her precious souls of the sea will be saved, before they are extinguished and lost forever.

*

The cruel sea has one more execution to perform. Paul is now mentally prepared to relinquish his life to its inevitable destiny. The moment of Leo's last heartbeat was also his last breath of hope. His source of strength and courage is now expended. He has no further resources to fight the agony of grief and despair. His mind is filled with intense darkness, without a single ray of hope to cling to. It is now utterly futile to contemplate thoughts of rescue or survival. It is time to submit to the Will of God, to trust in His mercy and deliverance. For six harrowing days and nights he has prayed for Divine Assistance. It was a cruel fate that not one moment of relief was granted, or one wish of comfort gratified. Paul now believes that from the moment his boat foundered, forcing them into the sea, they were all destined to die. They mistakenly believed that Divine Providence would organise their safe deliverance. It is a cruel irony that Paul now sees and understands the nature of the deliverance God had in mind. He accepts that the logic and meaning of God's ways are beyond human comprehension. His faith tells him we are only passing through this 'valley of tears' to our permanent home in Heaven. That consoling thought fortifies him as he waits his final call.

Leo is 'waked' lying on top of the raft of makeshift floats. It's a precariously unstable position. Paul has to constantly hold his body to prevent it slipping into the water. As long as he is alive he is determined to keep Leo from the ocean predators that would devour his little body in an instant. He ties small strips of polystyrene to his upper arms and also to his own. He knows that in a matter of hours, he will be joining Leo, Grandpa, Mario and Ali in a new eternal life. It will be a consolation to Gabriella and Dom, if their bodies can be found.

*

Jason and his team have now combed a vast area of the Mediterranean. Their search has covered a huge circle of the sea without the slightest trace of the 'St. Agatha' or her crew. Perplexed, frustrated and bitterly disappointed, Jason decides to return to their original starting point, the last recorded position of the boat.

It's mid-afternoon, the sea is calm and the sun is sizzling. The flotilla of vessels and weary eyes begin a new sweep of the gloomy sea. They will sail 50 miles towards Libya covering a width of ten miles. Jason is convinced they are now searching for survivors on a life raft. If the 'St. Agatha' was afloat, she would have been found. Their eyes are firmly focussed on the surface of the water for any tiny speck of hope that will reward their efforts and bring a happy ending to this agonising saga.

*

4.55 p.m. Major Tonio Bonnici, AFM, receives an urgent message. The Captain of the merchant ship 'Topaz' has sighted a body floating 58 nautical miles WSW off Malta. Major Bonnici immediately sends AFM P-51 patrol boat to the location to retrieve the body. The corpse will be taken ashore at Haywharf Base and transferred to Mater Dei Hospital for post mortem and identification.

*

Darkness descends like a shroud over Paul and his little stiff, cold son, as they drift aimlessly in the calm sea. Another long night of Limbo lies ahead. He is now oblivious to the isolation and hopelessness of his situation. He tries to stay awake but sleep is now impossible to resist. He dozes for a few minutes then wakes with a violent jerk, relieved to find Leo still with him. His own body is tied to the raft with a rope that has cut into his waist. It's painful, but it leaves his arms free to hold his son.

He doesn't even bother to search the circle of sea around him now. His eyes are too tired. His terrible hunger and thirst has eased, his mouth, tongue and throat are swollen and painful. His mind is confused and disorientated. His legs are cramped and numb. His strength is totally exhausted. He just wants to rest, sleep and die. He prays for a quick release from this exile of torment.

Jesus, Mary and Joseph, may I breathe forth my soul, in peace with you. Amen.

Wednesday

At one minute past nine, Major Bonnici, AFM Headquarters, receives a progress report from the police concerning the body recovered from the sea yesterday.

"A post mortem examination carried out this morning at Mater Dei Hospital, confirmed that death resulted from asphyxia, due to drowning. The body is that of a male, approximately 30 years of age. There are tattoos on both arms. The body fits the description of Mario Grima, Bluegarr Bay, a crewmember of the missing fishing boat, 'St Agatha'. Contact is presently being made with Mr Grima's mother to confirm a positive identification."

Major Bonnici requests a further report on completion of positive identification. He decides to withhold this preliminary information until the identity of the body is confirmed. Meanwhile, he orders all search resources to proceed to the area where the body was located.

*

Grace takes a little time to answer the doorbell. She is just finished her breakfast. Gingerly balancing herself behind the walking frame, she shuffles through the hallway to the door. The sight of two solemn-faced policemen startles her.

"We would like a word with you, Mrs Grima, please."

"Oh …Yes … Of course …Come in …Come in."

Seated in her neat sitting room, Grace listens as the young police officers gently explain why they have come. A body recovered from the sea yesterday may be that of her son.

"The body has arm tattoos and we need confirmation of the details of those tattoos for positive identification."

A feverish sensation overwhelms Grace. Cold sweat form in drops on her forehead, Her heart races, her body trembles, she is rendered speechless. She gestures with her hands, asking for time to recover her composure. Her sad eyes stare into space, her lips tremble in silent prayer.

The young policemen wait in dignified silence. She gradually recovers from the initial shock, dries her tear-filled eyes, gathers her thoughts.

"Yes, it's my son, Mario; my lovely son; my son in a million.

God has taken him; my only son, my only son."

Having received the details of the tattoos: a ship's anchor on one arm, a scroll with the word 'Grace' on the other, the police are satisfied that the identification is now confirmed. They offer thanks, sympathy, and leave.

Alone again, Grace reaches for her rosary beads. With a broken heart and eyes filled with tears, she begins;

"The First Sorrowful Mystery ...."

*

Gabriella receives a call from Major Bonnici informing her of the recovery of the body of Mario Grima and its positive identification. The news drives a spear through her heart. Her last hope is now gone. Throughout the long dismal week she has clung to an intuitive belief that somehow Paul would bring his boat and crew home safely. That hope is now shattered. Nothing will now dispel her clear conviction that they are all lost. She slumps into her brother's arms, sobbing in anguish.

*

The penetrating rays of the hot morning sun beam down on the primitive, floating bier, carrying its little corpse on top and a dying invalid in its wake. The warming atmosphere of the Mediterranean is of little benefit to Paul; the coldness of death is fast gathering over him. His sight is failing, he can no longer think clearly, fatigue is forcing him asleep; he can barely muster enough strength to hold Leo's body on the raft.

One thing he is now sure of. His sufferings are drawing to a close. His silent prayer is for a hasty release from this sea of heartbreak. He tussles against his heavy eyelids, against his sinking mind, He is losing the struggle to stay awake. He dozes into a delirious slumber – for how long, he has no idea. A sudden bolt of terror flashes through him. He senses impending disaster. He forces his eyes open. Leo! Where is Leo? He thrashes around with renewed feverish energy. The water reacts with rippling waves, the empty raft drifts quicker. The cruel reality impales Paul's troubled mind. **"Leo is gone!"**

*

Jason's task force is thirty miles off Libya on a frustrating, fruitless mission. He takes a satellite call from Kenneth Galea, secretary of the Fisheries Co-operative. Stunned and astounded, he asks Kenneth to repeat the devastating news.

"The Police have issued a statement."

'A body, now officially identified as Mario Grima, a crewmember of the 'St Agatha' was recovered from the sea yesterday at 5.30. P.m. by the AFM P-51 patrol boat, 58 nautical miles WSW off Malta. A post mortem carried out this morning at Mater Dei Hospital showed that death resulted from asphyxia, due to drowning. The body, which was in an advanced stage of decomposition, and had no identification *documents, was identified by tattoos, with the assistance of Mr Grima's mother.'*

Jason is furious with the AFM. Why did they not inform Kenneth yesterday evening, immediately the body was found? They agreed to tell the fishermen of any new developments. For the past twenty-four hours we have been searching 50 miles from where Mario was found. If we had known, we could have rushed there and by now, have found the others. Twenty hours has been lost and it will now take another four hours to get there. Troubled and angry, he radios the other skippers, turns and steams to the area, 58 nautical miles WSW off Malta.

*

It is almost 5.30 p.m. Jason and his search party have reached their target area. It's 24 hours since Mario's body was found. The fishermen are annoyed; lamenting the crucial lost hours. If they had known, they would have been here before dark yesterday. With so many boats searching, they would have found anything floating. Now it may be too late. Disturbed and frustrated, they begin their comb of the calm, blue sea.

Fifteen minutes into the search, Jason is on deck focusing intensely through his binoculars. He spots a helicopter ahead in the distant sky. It appears to be circling and hovering. He tells Angelo to accelerate, head for the chopper. The other boats will continue the slow, meticulous search. As 'The Blue Horizon' steams ahead at full power, Jason's heart is racing too. The helicopter is Italian, an AB212. The pilot has seen Jason approaching. He comes to meet him, turns and appears to lead him to the spot, then flies away. Jason, baffled and bewildered, continues on. Perhaps there is nothing there; a false alarm. Yes, there is something. The helicopter may have been out of fuel, leaving the scene to Jason.

A black speck develops into a floating body as panic-stricken Jason sails closer. The body, drifting face-downwards, appears swollen, bloated, and almost a metre above the water. Angelo steers the boat alongside the floating body. Jason's heart bursts into severe pounding, his mind into turmoil and grief. Through the clear blue water he recognises the contorted face of his father.

*

Paul has endured a long, sad day, semiconscious under a torturous sun. Since Leo slipped from his limp arms, into the lonely grave of the Mediterranean, his mind has refused to function. He just wants to die. To be reunited again with his father and son in Heaven, following their horrendous Purgatory would be a welcome release.

"Please God, make it happen soon."

He dozes into a delirious slumber. Restless, confused dreams are abruptly terminated in a sudden awakening to the cruel reality of his miserable existence. He knows that one of these slumbers will be the long one. His terrible physical pain is now gone, his mind is a thick fog, he is now oblivious to his inevitable fate. As the day fades into evening, Paul is convinced that the darkness now descending will shroud him for the last time. There will be no to-morrow. The thought, though percolating through a clouded mind, is still warm and soothing.

*

Gabriella is visiting a grieving, but resilient Grace. The cosy sitting room is crowded with neighbours and friends. They have come with solidarity and support, to share in the dignified mourning of a remarkable woman of faith. Food, drink and consoling words are present in abundance in an atmosphere of sadness, solace, and resignation to God's will. Grace will not accept pity, or allow thoughts of angry resentment enter her mind. Her prayers are now for the safe return to Gabriella of her husband and young son.

"I am old and my life is nearly over. But you need Paul. He is the breadwinner. Please God, he will be spared."

The little radio, standing on the windowsill in Grace's kitchen, is on continuously. The hourly news bulletins give updates of the sea search. Since yesterday afternoon, details of the recovery of Mario's body have been repeated many times. It's poignant content is endured by Grace in the hope that some hour it will also include good news about the other crewmembers.

"It's six o'clock. Here is the main evening news."

Gabriella and Grace move closer to the little radio.

"An unconfirmed report states that fishermen have, in the past hour, located a male body 60 nautical miles WSW of Malta, near where the body of Mario Grima was recovered yesterday. Early reports suggest the body may be another crewmember of the missing trawler, the 'St. Agatha'. It is being taken ashore by the AFM patrol boat P-52, and will be transferred to The Mater Dei Hospital for a post mortem examination."

The panic-filled eyes of Gabriella and Grace meet in a fusion of anguish, love and affection. They embrace in a tearful union of solidarity and sharing of this cruel adversity.

*

The AFM navel officers winch the badly decomposed body from the sea and gently place it on the deck of the P-52. The fishing boats gather in a semicircle to show respect and form a 'guard of honour'. Jason, watching from the deck of 'The Blue Horizon' has to be restrained to prevent him from open conflict with the navel officers. His mind is a combustion of rage, fuelled by heartfelt grief and mourning. To witness the appalling state of his father's body, bloated and contorted almost beyond recognition, to contemplate the agonising suffering and death he must have endured, has wounded Jason to the core. He is inconsolable with anguish, almost hysterical with bitter anger towards those responsible for the lost rescue hours.

As the P-52 begins the 60 miles voyage to Malta, the fishermen pause in a circle to reflect. Jason thoughts are recalling his life in the loving care and influence of a devoted father and mentor. Dad's vocation in life was working, caring and sharing. Wealth or status never interested him. He was a simple, honest, contented man, who loved his family, his God and his country. Jason will try to espouse those great characteristics and emulate the life of service, given so generously by his beloved father. That will be his mantra, a positive thought that gives him some little peace and consolation.

The fishermen, now rallying around Jason with sympathy and support, also grieve the loss of a genuine friend and true colleague. The sea has always been his workplace. He didn't have high education or academic degrees, but through dedication and hard work, became a master of his craft. His skill was recognised and respected, his generosity of spirit admired and appreciated. They will miss him, but they know that in Jason, and hopefully Paul, his legacy will live on.

Jason knows he can't afford to waste any more time in his dungeon of grief and anguish. Three more people are somewhere desperately waiting to be rescued. Each passing minute can be vital in their struggle for survival. He is more determined than ever to locate them and bring them home. His composure regained, his mind refocused, he tells his shipmates to resume the search.

"Move as fast as possible, without missing the slightest ripple or speck; it might be a person or a body."

He calls Gabriella on the satellite phone. He is surprised to find that she has already heard of the discovery of the body. For the past hour, since hearing the report on the radio, she has endured turmoil; not knowing its identity. Jason confirms her worse fears.

"It's Dad!"

The long agonising pause, linked through space, via satellite, from one broken heart to another, speaks louder than words. Back to the cruel reality of the present, two kindred spirits exchange heart-rending expressions of sorrow, solidarity and hope.

"Don't give up, Gabriella!"

Jason will not accept her assertion that they are all lost.

"We are searching. We will find them. I know we will."

Words, adequate to express her gratitude fail her.

"May God go with you."

As the boats are about to move off on their slow, painstaking search, Jason's eyes focus on a poignant but positive link that may lead him to the other stranded crewmembers. A narrow slick of oily, discoloured water extends westward from the point where his father's body was discovered. It's the body fluid trail, clearly visible on the surface of the mirror-calm sea. With mixed emotions, Jason decides to turn west and follow it. The other boats will follow in their organised formation behind him. Painfully retracing the drift path of his father's body, the trail is becoming less distinguishable, will soon dissipate completely. He will still continue in this direction, confident he is on the right track.

*

Paul is oblivious to the dismal, grey evening descending on him, drifting aimlessly through the blue-black dusk of his grim surroundings. His shrunken, withered body is rapidly fading into a welcome oblivion that will free him from this terrible abyss. His legs are numb, his head and face blistered and swollen. His tongue and throat are crusted and festered, his eyes tearless and closed. The rope tying him to the raft has eaten into the flesh of his waist, now septic and raw. His arms, burned and peeling, are weak and lifeless.

From extended periods, sedated in a restless, semiconscious stupor, he wakes for short flashes to grasp some little reality.

He is still alive. Still abandoned, isolated. Nothing has changed. Why doesn't God take him? Has he not endured enough Purgatory?

"Lord, please take me."

*

Night gently lowers its shroud of sombre gloom over the flotilla of sad, weary searchers, ending a day of emotional extremes. The warm sunlight is changed to a bleak, dismal dusk. Clear visibility is now a murky haze. Jason's tired eyes are still peering through the lens of his binoculars. Hours of deep concentration on empty grey water compounds his frustration and tiredness. It has been a soul-destroying day of turmoil and grief. His anger and mourning for his father is overshadowed by the vital imperative of finding the others. Reluctant to lower the binoculars as long as a flicker of light remains, he adjusts the lens for one last sweeping scan. Nothing to see but forlorn, grey water. Enlarging the scene for a final semicircle view, he suddenly gasps and yells as he spots something directly ahead. A smudge, darker than the surrounding water, about 500 metres away is looming into view. He fixes his gaze firmly on the dark patch. Approaching through the increasing darkness his heart begins to accelerate. The object appears to be some sort of floating raft. He signals to Angelo to stop. With naked eyes now, studying the primitive, floating object, Jason sees the outline of a human figure. It's a lifeless body attached to a makeshift raft. The boat eases closer. Jason is angry and distraught. Another tragic victim of the lost search hours. Almost upsides now, he screams a bloodcurdling cry. A hand has risen from the body, motioning a weak wave. He shouts to Angelo to radio the other boats to come quickly. Swimmers are needed to get the survivor on board. Removing his jacket, he dives into the dark sea, swims frantically to the raft.

"It's Paul ... He's alive."

*

Gabriella is oblivious to the plush décor and furniture as she sits in the waiting room of The Mater Dei Hospital. It's her first visit to the huge, new 'State of the Art' Medical Centre, opened just a few months ago. A massive investment and a wonderful facility for the people of Malta, but at 2 a.m. she is in no mood to admire the surroundings. It's been four tense hours since the helicopter winched Paul from the deck of the 'Blue Horizon', flying him here and straight to the theatre. She can't wait to hear that he is transferred back to the intensive care unit, and that she can now see him.

Since receiving the satellite phone call from Jason shortly after Paul was rescued, her mind has been a caldron of boiling emotions. Overpowering waves of ecstasy, agony, joy, sorrow, elation, and depression have consumed her. Her first prayers of gratitude to God were half-hearted and uttered with a questioning reservation. Thanks for the safe return of Paul, but why, after all the relentless prayers, did he need to take little Leo? Now, on tearful reflection, she is beginning to see some divine balance emerging. Perhaps her prayers *were* answered. It was a miracle that Paul was saved. Miracles don't just happen. Maybe God considered that in Paul's safe return, she has got a fair bargain, and her prayers were an important factor in securing that deal.

She feels like screaming with jubilation; wailing with bitter anguish. She does neither. Silently feeling guilt for her indulgence in self-pity, she thinks of Paul. What state must his mind be in? She can't even begin to comprehend the torture of mind and body that he has been through. She calms down. A feeling of heartfelt gratitude brings a soothing respite to her chaotic mind.

She thinks of Jason and the other boatmen, still out there on the lonely ocean searching for Ali's body and little Leo. Poor Jason, his heart must be broken, but still he will not give up. Finding his father's body in such a state would have broken most people. How did he have the strength to continue? To have soldiered on and rescued Paul was an example of true loyalty and courage.

The double doors swing open. Surgeon Abella, accompanied by

the Ward Sister of the intensive care unit, enter; Gabriella instinctively stands up.

"Your husband is a very lucky man, Mrs Gauci."

The surgeon is frank and forthright.

"Two hours longer in the water and he would have died. He is in bad shape. Lots of internal and external damage. He will need skin grafts to his legs and specialist treatment in the burns unit. We have stabilised him. He will be under intensive care for a few days. He will then have surgery, after which he will be transferred to the burns unit. He should make a full recovery, but will need time and lots of medication. Nurse will now take you down to see him."

"Thank you, Doctor."

Tiptoeing tentatively into the electronic cockpit of the private ward, Gabriella halts briefly to study the scene she has been mentally envisioning. Shocked and dismayed, she realises that nothing would have prepared her for this. Surrounded by a maze of ugly tubes and technology, Paul, sleeping in a haze of sedation, is unrecognisable, even to his wife. Swollen and blistered, his head and face seems to have emerged from an oven grill. His scabby eyes, peeling nose and black septic lips clearly reveal the extent of his ordeal. To see him alive after such devastation reinforces her belief in miracles. His pitiful features reminds her of another tortured face, one she has many times contemplated in times of sadness or sorrow. She sees a replica of the face of Jesus at the foot of the cross, after *His* suffering and crucifixion.

As if sensing her presence, Paul eases his eyes open to reveal the heavenly gift of his wife's loving face. Disoriented and confused, his brave attempt at speaking comes out as incoherent mumbling. Gabriella's efforts to express her feelings are even less successful She is too overwhelmed with pure, unbridled emotions of gratitude and love. Manoeuvring through pipes and attachments she leans over him clasping him in a tender embrace.

In a precious, treasured silence, charged with intense love, passion and poignancy, two divided, tortured souls are one again. A moment of bittersweet emotion, that will linger in their memory for the rest of their lives.

Words are not required.

✳✳✳

Epilogue

The searing power of the summer sun has now lost its intensity. The brown, arid landscape has acquired a soft green tinge. The lampuki have come and gone. Six mournful months has not assuaged the gloom and despondency that still hangs over Bluegarr Bay.

Four souls of the sea are still vivid images in the minds and memory of the fishing folk. The circumstances of their tragic demise lives on to haunt, with questions that may never be answered. An official government enquiry is meticulously 'snailing' through the evidence and will eventually report. The fishermen will not name and blame, or look for convictions and resignations - only the truth and assurances for the future.

Still hurting with the constant reminder that having recovered the three adults, they failed to find the little boy, who still remains at sea. Though accepting the cruel fact that his grave will now be the ocean, his serene face of innocence will forever be lovingly etched in the hearts and minds of this little fishing community.

*

The picturesque setting of the little graveyard, on a plateau overlooking the harbour is where Paul, Gabriella and Dom have come to pray, contemplate and remember.

Paul's physical health is slowly improving as each day goes by; his emotions, still resisting the healing of time, remain disturbed, damaged and depressed.

The trauma and devastation of his ordeal, the litany of unanswered questions, the skipper's guilt for his lost crew, are all sinister ghosts, still loitering menacingly in his mind. Perhaps time will exorcise them, leaving a clear, unhindered gateway to the future. Perhaps his chart still contains further unpredictable graphs. Perhaps, but that's for another day. For now, he takes one day at a time, trying to consign yesterday to history, to-morrow to God.

Dom is missing more than a brother and grandfather. Part of him has gone with them. Unable to express in words the seismic upheaval to his little world, he is soothed by the comfort his Dad's everyday home presence brings. The care and nurturing of his parents, hitherto shared, is now all his - another little token to ease the pain.

Gabriella's heart has a compartment devoted exclusively to her little lost son. A shrine she visits every passing hour, it is adorned with every image of his serene face, providing comfort and sorrow in equal measure. The gift of Paul's return is now appreciated with sincere gratitude for the miracle it was. Her prayers of thanksgiving will mark each day for the rest of her life.

The little wounded family kneels in silent prayer by the graveside of Grandpa. The beautiful new marble headstone is designed for two. Perhaps another miracle may yet fill the second grave. Grandpa would approve.

Until then, the 'Confirmation Day' photograph of Grandpa and Leo, engraved in a ceramic frame on the headstone, will testify to their special love – *'On Earth, as it is now in Heaven.'*

SPARE RIDE
Paddy Cummins

Jenny seemed to have everything.

Fearless and talented in the saddle. Brilliantly distinguished in the boardroom. Beautiful and sensational in the bedroom. She was still unfulfilled, searching. Why? Her handsome, older, doting husband, Dr. Ken McKevitt, knew the answer. Devastated by his failure, consumed with intense possessive love, he tried desperately to hold on to her.

Gary Wren, a stunning young racehorse trainer had just 'arrived' in the beautiful Green Valley of South Kilkenny. Fate played its devastating hand in locking all three together in an intriguing and turbulent saga, winning Jenny her greatest prize; her husband his peace of mind.

The reward was great, but the cost was even greater.

***

Bridge Publishing
www.bridgepublishing.net

GREEN LODGE
Paddy Cummins

The equine bloodlines developed by Janet Johnson at Green Lodge Stud Farm are the secret of her brilliant success.

Her human bloodlines are a secret too, but they would lead her to turmoil, strife and dismal failure. The dream of nineteen-year-old, penniless, stable lad, Ricky Baker, to one day own a stud farm, takes an unexpected turn with the chance discovery that his wealthy Farmer/Politician boss, is not the Sam McArdy he thought he was.

It is the first step on a journey that would lead him to Gillian and change their lives forever.

So begins two years of adventure, excitement, ecstasy, passion, pain and torment.

His dream and Gillian's true love are the powerful strengths that bring them through.

***

Bridge Publishing
www.bridgepublishing.net

Also by
Paddy Cummins

At Home in Ireland

Spare Ride

Green Lodge

Shades of Life

Fields of Green

The Bombing of Campile

Bridge Publishing
www.bridge